Alice-Miranda
in Hollywood

Books by Jacqueline Harvey

Alice-Miranda
in Hollywood

Jacqueline Harvey

RANDOM HOUSE AUSTRALIA

A Random House book
Published by Penguin Random House Australia Pty Ltd
Level 3, 100 Pacific Highway, North Sydney NSW 2060
www.penguin.com.au

Penguin
Random House
Australia

First published by Random House Australia in 2017

Addresses for the Penguin Random House group of companies can be found at
global.penguinrandomhouse.com/offices.

National Library of Australia
Cataloguing-in-Publication entry

Creator: Harvey, Jacqueline, author
Title: Alice-Miranda in Hollywood/Jacqueline Harvey
ISBN: 978 0 14378 061 8 (paperback)
Series: Harvey, Jacqueline. Alice-Miranda; 16
Target audience: For primary school age
Subjects: Friendship – Juvenile fiction
             Travel – Juvenile fiction
             Motion pictures – Juvenile fiction
             Hollywood (Los Angeles, Calif.) – Juvenile fiction

Cover and internal illustrations by J.Yi
Cover design by Mathematics www.xy-1.com
Typeset in 13/18 pt Adobe Garamond by Midland Typesetters, Australia
Printed in Australia by Griffin Press, an accredited ISO AS/NZS 14001:2004
Environmental Management System printer

Penguin Random House Australia uses papers that are natural, renewable
and recyclable products and made from wood grown in sustainable forests.
The logging and manufacturing processes are expected to conform to the
environmental regulations of the country of origin.

*For Ian and Olivia, and for Sandy,
who I know would have loved a little
Hollywood magic*

Prologue

His wife's voice echoed up the stairs. She was calling his name and muttering about where he could have got to this time. He knew that she'd exhausted all avenues in the garden, having spotted her charging about, poking her head into every nook and cranny. To be fair, it was usually where she found him. There was something therapeutic about raking leaves and trimming hedges, although it often got him into trouble for interfering in Eduardo's domain.

She called again with greater urgency, reminding him they were to be at dinner by seven. The old man sighed. His wife was never late for anything. She was never early either – according to her, that would be even worse. She was always on time and, while it made her renowned for having the most impeccable manners in Hollywood, it drove him to distraction. Just once he wanted to arrive half an hour after the appointed time. He looked down at his yard clothes. They were hardly shabby, but there was no way he was going to be allowed off the premises wearing them. Besides, it wasn't worth going to war over a change of shirt and trousers.

He turned over the photograph in his hand and gazed at the familiar swirls of his handwritten inscription. It had been such a happy time, until everything changed in a split second. His entire universe altered by one terrible mistake. There wasn't a day that he didn't think about how different things could have been, but there was no point living in the past. She was gone. He'd made the best of it, really, and now there was one more thing he had to do. Then perhaps he would find some peace. For all of them.

He carefully put away the picture, locking the small wooden box inside the cupboard. He flicked off the light and slid back the panel, then entered the main part of the attic, glancing at one of the glass cabinets and nodding a silent acknowledgement. He could hear her footsteps on the stairs and those heaving sighs that deigned trouble ahead.

Chapter 1

Alice-Miranda splayed her fingers and grinned at her baby cousins. 'Boo!' she exclaimed, sending them flying to the other end of the playroom. It was a beautiful space with the ceiling painted to look like the sky, complete with fluffy clouds. One wall comprised a giant chalkboard while the others boasted hand-painted scenes of famous landmarks from around the world. There was a craft station, child-sized couches and a library too. The best part, though, was the giant pirate ship in the centre, which the children could climb aboard and hide inside. Marcus and Imogen often spent hours playing with one another, but at that moment they only had eyes for Millie.

The twins giggled uncontrollably as they chased after the girl, who was leaping about and doing forward rolls. Alice-Miranda was laughing so hard she felt as if her sides were about to split. She couldn't think of a more beautiful sound than the tinkling of the toddlers' laughter, nor remember a time when her heart had felt fuller. Neither of the older girls saw Alice-Miranda's aunt sneak into the room and start filming.

'No more,' Millie gasped between giggles.

'Again!' Marcus demanded. He stood astride the girl's belly and sat down with a triumphant thump.

'Come here, buster,' Alice-Miranda said, sweeping the cheeky boy into her arms. 'Poor Millie. You've knocked the wind out of her.'

Charlotte paused the recording and chuckled. 'Goodness me, you're a brute. You need to be gentle, my darling man,' she said in soothing tones.

Alice-Miranda spun around and smiled. 'How long have you been standing there, Aunt Charlotte?'

'Long enough.' Charlotte waggled her phone at the girl. 'This should be good value for the twenty-first birthday vault.'

'More,' Imogen pleaded, scrabbling to take her brother's place. Her big brown eyes, framed by a forest of long lashes, blinked innocently as she did her best to persuade Millie to restart the game.

'No way, Jose,' Millie said, rolling over onto her stomach and resting her chin in her hands. 'You two are rougher than the Downsfordvale hockey team.'

Not one to be deterred, Imogen sat down on the girl's bottom in protest.

Millie scrunched up her nose and looked around at the toddler. 'Did someone just do something evil in their nappy?'

'Poo poo,' Imogen replied, as if it were the sweetest thing in the world.

'A very smelly one,' Millie agreed, trying desperately to fan away the toxic fumes.

Marcus pulled a face and imitated Millie's hand movements. 'Poo poo!'

'I don't think you can talk, young man,' Charlotte said. 'Not after what I dealt with this morning. Girls, would you mind taking Marcus to the kitchen while I get Imi changed?'

Alice-Miranda and Millie nodded, eager to help while Charlotte disappeared into the house with her daughter. Millie held Marcus's hand as they walked down the long hall from the playroom to the kitchen at the back of the house. The smell of garlic and tomatoes filled the air.

'Hola Magdalena,' Alice-Miranda said cheerfully. She paused and breathed in the delightful aromas of the woman's cooking. 'Mmm, dinner smells delicious.'

A woman with dark wavy hair popped up from the other side of the island and placed some bowls on the benchtop. Her brown eyes sparkled like stars as she smiled at the children. *'Hola chicas!'* she exclaimed, waving with her hips. 'It is my very especial chilli con carne, but no need to worry – it is not too hot for your delicate tongues. I have to train up the babies' tastebuds one small step at a time. When you are from Oaxaca, Mexico, it is simply part of life to eat the fire.'

The girls grinned and Millie lifted Marcus into his highchair. Charlotte reappeared with a powdery-smelling Imogen, who she strapped in beside her brother at the enormous marble-topped island bench.

'I still can't believe we're here.' Alice-Miranda sighed happily, as she did her best to catch the globs of meat that were falling from Imogen's face. Despite Alice-Miranda and Millie having wrestled a couple of bibs over the toddlers' heads, it was only a matter of minutes before they were both wearing as much chilli as they'd consumed. 'It's so lovely to have some time with you and the twins, Aunt Charlotte.'

'To think it's all because of Caprice.' Millie shook her head. 'Who knew there was a generous bone in *that* girl's body.'

'To be fair, I think Caprice has made an effort to get on with people this past term,' Alice-Miranda said. 'She's been helping Mia with her homework twice a week and she volunteered for the village beautification project, which we know from experience means getting your hands dirty and then some. She told me she thought you were very brave when I had my accident too.'

Millie rolled her eyes. 'She never said anything to me, but I guess she has been a lot less horrible.'

'Well, I am very glad to hear that Caprice made mention of her friends to the agent,' Charlotte said. 'Although I suspect the studio's willingness to allow you all to audition might have had something to do with her mother agreeing to record a television special for them while she's here.'

Millie looked over in mock horror. 'Gee, I thought we got the parts because of our extraordinary talents.'

Charlotte's cheeks lit up. 'Oh, Millie, I didn't mean it like that,' she said, mortified. 'Of course they wouldn't have asked you to be in it if they didn't think you were up to the task. And the bonus is that I get to have children in the house who can do more than babble and blow raspberries.'

In the middle of last term, Alice-Miranda and Millie could hardly believe their luck when they'd been invited, along with several of their friends, to take on small roles in Lawrence Ridley's upcoming movie, *Frontier Woman: The Life and Times of Nellie Williams*. They were even more surprised to learn that it was Caprice who had made it happen. A talent scout had heard her singing at the National Eisteddfod and recommended her to one of the casting agents, as the movie was an old-fashioned Hollywood musical set in the Wild West. When Caprice found out that Lawrence Ridley was signed on to play the lead, she happened to mention that she was best friends with his niece. One thing led to another and, before anyone knew it, several of the children had landed parts, largely due to their being involved in the Winchester-Fayle Singers. Auditions were held at the school and you can only imagine how excited Mr Lipp and Mr Trout were at the prospect of being involved in a Hollywood production.

But there had been one hitch – the shooting schedule had to align with the school break. While Miss Grimm and Professor Winterbottom recognised the value of such an experience, neither was keen for the children to travel during term time, particularly as the film was to be shot on a sound stage in Los Angeles and on location at the Grand Canyon. Millie had huffed about it for weeks, complaining that Miss Grimm was just in a bad mood because she was pregnant and her ankles were swollen, but all was forgotten when the plans fell into place. While the adult cast had three months of filming, the children only had ten days. Hence, there was no room for mess-ups if they were to be done in the allotted time.

Poor Mr Trout had been set to accompany the children with Mr Lipp when, at the eleventh hour, he was struck down with a bout of pneumonia and rushed to hospital. Fortunately, it was arranged that the children would be supervised on set by the first assistant director and would stay with Alice-Miranda's

Aunt Charlotte and Uncle Lawrence. Mr Trout was terribly disappointed to miss out, and Alice-Miranda had already decided she'd take a special souvenir home to cheer him up. Alice-Miranda and Millie had flown to Los Angeles with Charlotte and the twins, who had been visiting at Highton Hall until the end of term. The others were due to arrive a day later.

'I'm looking forward to meeting this new and improved version of Caprice,' Charlotte said. 'I've invited Venetia to base herself here too. She and Caprice will have the guesthouse above the garages.'

Millie's face dropped.

The wooden spoon Magdalena was using to stir the chilli clattered on the kitchen tiles as the woman spun around and pressed her palms together. 'Oh my Lord in heaven above, Missus Charlotte, you did not tell me that! How will I possibly cook for *the* Missus Baldini? She is my idol.'

'She is really lovely,' Alice-Miranda confirmed. 'And completely down-to-earth.'

'Unlike her daughter, whose head is in the clouds,' Millie mumbled.

Magdalena fanned herself with one hand and steadied herself against the bench with the other. 'Oh, Missus Charlotte, I am overcoming with nerves.

Who am I to prepare even a glass of water for the great Venetia Baldini?'

Millie rushed around with a chair for the woman, who held onto the arms while lowering herself down gently.

'Your cooking is magnificent, Magdalena. I've never tasted guacamole as good as yours anywhere in the world, and your home-made corn chips are to die for,' Alice-Miranda assured her. 'I'm hoping that you can give me your mole poblano recipe too so I can pass it on to Mrs Oliver.'

The woman tried hard not to smile. 'Miss Alice-Miranda, you are far too kind, but I am not a cook's spatula compared to Missus Baldini.'

'Magdalena, you can hold your own with any chef I've ever known,' Charlotte scolded. 'And I'm sure Venetia will be nothing but gracious about your food. Take the opportunity to show off to your heart's content. Anyway, it would only be for a few days and then the children and Lawrence will be away on location, all things going to plan.'

Millie jiggled on the spot with excitement. 'I can't wait! I was reading that the Grand Canyon is one thousand eight hundred metres deep. That's almost two whole kilometres! And the rock found at the very bottom is around two *billion* years old. Grandpa bought me another guide book so I can bore everyone's socks off.'

'I remember the first time I saw it,' Charlotte said. 'I couldn't speak. Your mother and I went there as girls with your grandparents and I was completely overwhelmed. It's stunning.'

'And not in the least boring,' Alice-Miranda added.

'I just hope no one sleepwalks.' Millie gulped.

Magdalena shook her head and stood up to resume her stirring. 'Miss Millie, you are scaring my pants off.'

'Did you know the Grand Canyon is one of the seven natural wonders of the world?' Alice-Miranda said.

'Along with Mount Everest and Victoria Falls and the northern lights and three other places I can't remember,' Millie said. 'Maybe when we finish school we can go on a gap year and visit them all. We do travel pretty well together.'

Alice-Miranda smiled. 'Sounds like a perfect plan, Millie.'

'Good luck getting your parents to agree to that,' Charlotte said with a chuckle. Although she knew very well that her niece was one of the most persuasive people in the world, and once Alice-Miranda had made up her mind about something there was no stopping her.

'Mummy and Daddy will be fine,' Alice-Miranda said. 'But perhaps we should get some weekend jobs to start saving up.'

Millie shrugged. 'We're getting paid for the movie, so that's a start.'

Charlotte regarded the twins, who seemed to have got chilli con carne into just about every orifice. 'I think it's bath time for you lot.'

'I'll run it,' Alice-Miranda offered, hopping off her stool.

Millie grinned. 'Why don't we use the garden hose?'

'That's probably a much better idea,' Charlotte said, rolling her eyes as Marcus stuffed another piece of mincemeat up his nose.

Chapter 2

The bubbly Finkelstein's shop assistant asked who the book was for, catching Tyger off guard. Without a second's hesitation, the woman conjured an eight-year-old daughter's birthday present. She felt silly for lying, but reading middle-grade fiction had been a guilty pleasure all her life and she wasn't about to stop now. Besides, she'd been dying to get her hands on the latest J L Harvey and, given today was actually her birthday, she'd treated herself to the book and was looking forward to lunch at one of her favourite restaurants.

Tyger Lombardi wandered through the department store, stopping to admire a hat when she realised that Alexa Mills, one of the biggest stars in Hollywood, was just across the way in the make-up department, sampling lipsticks. If only she had her camera with her. Any shot of Alexa Mills, no matter how mundane, was worth something. Tyger reminded herself it was her birthday and resisted the temptation to snap a picture on her phone. She didn't want to risk a scene if anyone saw her and, surely, she could have one day off.

Tyger walked out of the department store and down to the restaurant on street level. She had made a reservation and was swiftly shown to her table among the busy lunchtime crowd. Tyger sat down and, for the first time in ages, paid scant attention to anyone else. Instead, she pored over the menu and decided on the tagliatelle. She knew her friend Katie would have the ravioli and hopefully she'd get the cheque too, given the current state of Tyger's bank balance.

It wasn't long before her friend barrelled through the door, a flurry of apologies sputtering from her lips as she bustled over to the table. Katie was in such a tizz that she didn't see the waiter with his tray of drinks. There was a bump and a crash, the collision sending glasses into the air before they shattered on the floor. Heads turned and several diners gasped, but the liquids seemed to miss everyone, though some of the bags sitting on the floor weren't so fortunate. Tyger grimaced.

Katie's hands flew to her mouth. 'I'm such a klutz, darling. Lunch is on me.' She rolled her eyes and kissed Tyger's cheek. 'Happy birthday, hun.'

Within seconds there were at least five staff members cleaning up the mess. Tyger didn't realise that her handbag and shopping had copped a spray, along with the belongings of other diners as well. One of the waitstaff swiftly scooped up the bags and whisked them away to be dried, returning the items to their places before anyone had time to notice.

Tyger shifted in her seat and tried to enjoy her birthday. A number of diners had been glancing in her direction since the kerfuffle. She hoped she hadn't offended any of them with her photos lately, although there were a few faces she suspected she might have. Being a member of the paparazzi in this town was not easy, even on your birthday.

Chapter 3

Aviva Goldberg licked her fingers, then pressed them firmly on the rogue strand of hair that was sticking up at the back of her son's head. The dry Californian air did nothing to help matters.

'Mum, please stop that,' the boy whispered, batting her away and connecting with one of the large rocks on her left hand. 'Ow!'

'Booboola, it's your very first day on set. I just want you to look your best.' The woman tapped the tip of his nose. 'We will make a movie star of you yet.'

Sasha Goldberg swallowed hard. Never in a million years would he have thought that he'd get the part. It was the last thing he wanted. Trouble was, he couldn't back out now.

In stark contrast to her son, Aviva Goldberg possessed all the self-assurance in the world. She was as glitzy as her name suggested and nurtured a penchant for anything and everything that sparkled. It was a well-known fact among the boutique owners of Beverly Hills that, if it glinted and shimmered, Aviva would buy it – in large. Unlike most of the women in Hollywood, Aviva embraced her ampleness. She was well aware of the jibes from some of her so-called friends, but it didn't matter. They weren't married to Eli Goldberg, son of the most powerful studio boss in town – and her husband was certain to be taking over soon; her father-in-law was positively ancient.

Aviva almost pushed her son through the door of the sound stage. Inside, the vast building had been transformed into a town in the Wild West, complete with a saloon bar, assay office, mercantile and schoolhouse. It looked like something one would have encountered in the California Gold Rush of the 1800s.

A young woman wearing a headset hurried over to the pair. She was glad she'd bothered to make an effort with her appearance today, but even in her favourite black cigar pants and pink cashmere sweater (that had cost her a week's rent), she still felt like a peasant in the presence of her boss's wife. 'Good morning, Mrs Goldberg. How are you feeling, Sasha?'

The boy's cheeks burned as they tended to do whenever he was anxious. 'Okay, I suppose.'

'You've got nothing to worry about. It's only rehearsals today,' the woman said with an encouraging smile.

'Don't bother, Emmy,' Aviva sighed. 'I already told him that, but he gets so worked up. That son of mine does not appreciate his own talents.'

Emmy nodded absently as she spotted another mother and son wandering around the set. 'Oh, Blade, Mrs Crawford,' she called, waving to them. 'I'd like you to meet Sasha and Mrs Goldberg.'

Sasha turned towards his co-star. Even from a distance he could see how tall and good-looking the boy was. His appearance did nothing to quell the mounting unease in Sasha's stomach. It was probably nerves, further exacerbated by the three jam doughnuts he'd scoffed after his breakfast. Most people lost their appetite when they were nervous, but not Sasha. He just ate more. However, unlike his mother, he never gained a pound. Sasha gave a weak wave and shook hands with the lad, wincing at his grip.

'Sorry,' the boy said, noticing Sasha's distress. 'I've been in training for months.'

Sasha's eyes widened. 'For what?' he asked.

Blade casually raised an eyebrow. 'The stunts, of course.'

Sasha looked at his mother, his red face glowing brighter. 'I don't have to do my own stunt work, do I?'

Aviva patted her son's cheeks. 'Of course not, booboola.'

Sasha pulled away from her. He could feel Blade's smirk even though he didn't dare look at the boy. The idea of performing his own stunts filled Sasha with a fear and loathing even greater than the prospect of being force-fed brussels sprouts. There was absolutely no way he was going to ride along any of those narrow Grand Canyon trails, let alone gallop on a horse anywhere. Then again, he thought, an injury would get him out of filming altogether.

He pondered this for a few seconds, then concluded that falling off a horse would hurt and he hated pain too. It was right up there with green vegetables and horses.

Meanwhile, Aviva introduced herself to Blade's mother and swiftly guided the woman away from the boys. 'I'm so pleased that Sasha is going to have a friend on set. He's a little shy – his father and I cannot for the life of us work out why. It's not a trait that runs in our family, that's for sure.' She sighed and shrugged her shoulders. 'He has a gift that simply cannot be denied. We're thrilled that he's earned himself this part. His grandfather was so surprised I think he almost fell off his chair. Anyway, it will be good for Sasha to spend time with someone his own age. I assume Blade is also twelve?'

Tish Crawford nodded grudgingly. She had thought Sasha ten at most. 'Yes, but Blade is very mature for his age,' she said in a loud voice. 'He's been acting since before he could walk.'

Sasha felt the world shrinking in on him. What gift? Acting wasn't his thing at all – he'd only auditioned because his grandmother had insisted and he'd been sure he wouldn't stand a chance. This kid – Blade – had the kind of seriously Hollywood name an actor should have and, to make matters worse, he had years of experience too. Sasha had no doubt that Blade was going to make him look like an even bigger fool than he already felt.

'What other movies have you done?' Blade asked, sounding bored. He seemed much more interested in how three crew members were attaching a set of steps to the saloon.

'None,' Sasha replied in a small voice.

'Really?' Blade's jaw dropped open in disbelief. 'So, you don't know how anything works?'

'Well, I've been on sets before, but –'

'Excuse me, everyone,' Emmy said, walking back to the group with a woman and young girl in tow, 'let me introduce you to Caprice and her mum. Caprice will be playing the role of young Nellie.'

Blade glanced over at them and was immediately overcome with an extremely discomforting feeling. The girl's long silky hair cascaded past her shoulders like a river of molten copper and her eyes were the most dazzling shade of sapphire blue. When she smiled it was as if the lights had been turned up a notch. Blade gulped.

'Oh my gawd!' Aviva squawked. 'Venetia Baldini – you are a goddess in our home! My husband adores your pineapple passionfruit pavlova and there's only one person who's even more in love with your food and you're looking right at him.' She pointed at Sasha, whose face went from blush pink to chilli red in less than a second. 'I'm Aviva Goldberg and this is my son, Sasha. He's got the lead boy role in the movie.'

Caprice rolled her eyes. 'What part do you have?' she asked Blade.

'I'm Nellie's cousin,' he rasped, his mouth suddenly as dry as cotton wool.

'Oh, that's a great character,' Caprice said, inspecting her newly manicured fingernails. 'Pity it's such a small role. No one will have time to notice you.'

Tish eyeballed the girl. 'It's not necessarily about the quantity, young lady. I can assure you the quality will be exceptional.'

'Um, sorry to interrupt, but we've got to get you lot to wardrobe before the run-through,' Emmy said. 'And there's Sophie.' She gave the girl a wave. 'She's playing the role of your little sister, Caprice.'

Caprice couldn't help thinking the girl reminded her of Alice-Miranda, with her long chocolate curls and dark eyes, but she seemed quite shy. Emmy introduced Sophie Roussos and her father, Anthony, to the group. Unlike Aviva and Tish, the man was in a hurry to get away, telling them he was due at a meeting in the city. He kissed his daughter's cheek and bid them all farewell.

Emmy led the group out of the sound stage and across to a smaller building. At the door, she stopped and faced the mothers. 'Sorry, ladies,' she said firmly, 'but no parents allowed from this point. I'll call you when they're half an hour from finishing.'

Tish's eyebrows knitted together. 'But I always watch Blade's rehearsals.'

Aviva began to push her way through the door. 'And I really don't think Sasha is ready to be left on his own.'

'I'm afraid I'm under strict instructions,' Emmy insisted, smiling tersely, 'from the executive producer.'

Aviva stopped and frowned. 'But that's . . . that's my husband. He can't do that!'

Eli Goldberg zoomed past in a golf cart. 'I can and I just did, darling. It's much better this way,' he called, blowing her a kiss.

Aviva stood frozen to the spot, her mouth flapping like a dying goldfish as the children disappeared inside the building with Emmy. You could almost see the smoke pouring out of the woman's ears.

'Why don't we go and get a coffee?' Venetia suggested, a tad too brightly. 'I've heard about a place down on Sunset where the macarons are world-renowned.'

'Oh my gawd, I love macarons,' Aviva gasped, instantly forgetting her son.

'Clearly,' Tish muttered under her breath. It was going to be a long shoot.

Chapter 4

Santa Monica Boulevard ran for miles, from Beverly Hills to the coast with an endless motorcade of fancy cars. There were shiny convertibles as well as old makes, such as Cadillacs and Buicks, all with smartly dressed drivers. It was a sparkling afternoon and Charlotte had decided to take Alice-Miranda, Millie and the twins to visit the Santa Monica Pier.

'I didn't realise it was a funfair,' Millie said, as she craned her neck to see the rides further along the boardwalk that jutted out into the ocean.

'Oh, the Santa Monica Pier is world-famous,' Charlotte said. 'And one of the first places Lawrence took me on a date. I love it here.'

The girls helped to unload the babies as Charlotte pulled their double stroller out of the car. The twins were soon strapped in and ready to go. They babbled away to each other while Millie and Alice-Miranda's eyes lit up at the rides and old-fashioned fairground attractions inside Pacific Park.

The group stopped at a colourful booth lined with balloons.

'Roll up, roll up,' a man in a baseball cap spruiked. 'Come try your hand at bursting my balloons. There are prizes galore!'

Millie looked at Alice-Miranda and raised her eyebrows. 'It's like taking candy from a baby.' Millie picked up a dart and eyed the target. She rocked back and forth, took a deep breath and launched the missile, popping a green balloon with a loud bang. The twins squealed and clapped their hands. Alice-Miranda cheered.

'Well done, sweetheart!' Charlotte said, patting Millie on the back.

Millie missed on her second attempt, but hit a red balloon on her third. The man winked and handed over an elephant and a shark toy, much to the delight of Imogen and Marcus.

Millie grinned. 'Told you it was easy.'

'You're amazing,' Alice-Miranda said, as the two girls linked arms and discussed what to try next.

They decided on the roller-coaster followed by the ferris wheel. Charlotte took the twins over to watch a young man make balloon animals, which kept them happy until the girls returned. Together, they went for ice-cream and a ride on the famous carousel inside the Looff Hippodrome at the end of the pier. Alice-Miranda sat holding Imogen tight in a little car on the inner ring of the merry-go-round. Charlotte was opposite her with Marcus and they all watched Millie bobbing up and down on one of the gorgeous carved ponies. She was pretending to be a jockey and had the lot of them in fits of laughter as she stood up in the stirrups and urged the beast to go faster.

Afterwards, the twins dozed while Charlotte pointed out the lifeguard towers and the cycle path that went all the way to Venice Beach and beyond.

'I love it here,' Millie gushed wistfully.

Alice-Miranda gave her aunt a squeeze around the middle. 'Thank you for bringing us.'

'Oh, darling, it was a pleasure,' Charlotte said, hugging her back.

As they reached the car, a woman's voice shouted loudly, 'Hey, Charlotte!'

The girls looked up to see a long camera lens pointed at them.

Charlotte gasped and practically threw the twins into their car seats while Millie and Alice-Miranda bundled the stroller into the boot. Imogen began to cry, which set off her brother.

'Hop in, girls, and whatever you do, don't look at her,' Charlotte instructed. She turned the ignition and soon enough they were out of the car park and onto the street.

'Who was that?' Millie asked, twisting around in her seat to check that there were no suspicious vehicles following them.

'She's a horrible paparazzo called Tyger Lombardi and she has no ethics whatsoever,' Charlotte said. 'She took photographs of me and the children when I was putting them to bed one night. She hid in a tree on the grass verge in front of the house and must have had an extremely powerful lens. I stupidly hadn't closed the curtains, but then again, the house is set quite a long way back from the road and is surrounded by a very private fence; it was the last thing I ever expected to happen.'

'That's terrible,' Alice-Miranda said.

Millie was aghast. 'Why would she do that?' she asked.

'Lawrence and I were being really careful about not having the children's photographs out in public, so the first pictures were always going to be worth a ridiculous amount of money. We wanted to protect them from all that nonsense for as long as we could,' Charlotte explained. 'In hindsight, we probably should have released some photos just so no one would have cared.'

Alice-Miranda shook her head. 'Some of those photographers have no manners at all. Aunty Gee has problems with them constantly, and I remember when Jacinta's mother used to get stalked for pictures too. She was always in *Gloss and Goss*, which used to upset Jacinta no end.'

Millie looked at her quizzically. 'It's understandable with Aunty Gee – she is the Queen, and I thought Ambrosia loved it.'

'She might have once, but her life has changed completely now and so has she,' Alice-Miranda replied. 'It's sad, isn't it, that because someone's famous, everyone thinks they're fair game. I suppose in some ways it comes with the job, but it sounds as though Miss Lombardi takes it way too far.'

'Precisely,' Charlotte said, thrumming her fingers on the steering wheel and glancing in the rear-vision mirror. 'I was so horrified when I saw the photographs in *Stars Weekly*, I went straight to the police and they were able to get an injunction before Tyger could sell them to the rest of the world.'

'Should you report her to the police now?' Alice-Miranda asked.

Charlotte sighed. 'Honestly, they can't do much about her and we were in a public place. Fortunately, there aren't too many like her. She's just a leech.'

'Or a tiger,' Millie said, forming claws with her hands. 'Always ready to pounce when you least expect it.' She growled and pretended to launch at the twins, who in a split second stopped their grizzling and were squealing with delight.

None of them noticed the silver hatchback changing lanes behind them. Tyger was planning to catch up to Charlotte at a red light and, with the dark tinting on her windows, the woman wouldn't even know the pictures had been taken until the deed was well and truly done.

Chapter 5

Lucas Nixon guided his friends into the family room of the Beverly Hills mansion the Ridley-Highton-Smith family called home. Jacinta, Sep and Sloane scanned the expansive room, taking it all in. The huge area included a white Hampton's-style kitchen in the centre as well as a seating area with plush couches and a television mounted above a stone fireplace at the far end. There was a dining table for twelve and another sitting area. The back wall of the house comprised the largest set of bi-fold doors the children had ever seen. They opened on to a flagstone patio with white wicker furniture and another fireplace. Muted grey walls were bordered by crisp white ceilings and woodwork. The house resembled a scene within the pages of a magazine, beautifully decorated but cosy and comfortable too.

'Hello,' Lucas called. 'Is anyone home?' This was not quite the welcome he'd been expecting.

Seconds later, Magdalena rushed out of the butler's pantry. 'Master Lucas!' she gasped, pinching his cheeks. 'Oh, my gorgeous boy, look how much you have grown! I am shrinking beside you. Now, you will introduce me to your friends, but I think . . .' Magdalena paused and considered Jacinta. 'You must be the famous Miss Headlington-Bear. You are even more beautiful than Lucas told me.' Magdalena took Jacinta's hands in hers and gave them a squeeze.

Sloane and Sep did their best not to laugh. Lucas had mentioned more than once that Magdalena was a colourful character, but right at the minute, there seemed to be a competition between Lucas and Jacinta to see whose face could turn the reddest.

Hoping to ease their friends' embarrassment, Sep and Sloane introduced themselves to the family cook and each received a hug.

'Oh, my Father God in heaven, you are all gorgeous children,' Magdalena fizzed. 'Come, you must tell me everything about yourselves. Who would like some afternoon tea? I have my especial chocolate cake with a sprinkle of chilli.' Magdalena waggled her eyebrows.

'Yes!' Lucas clenched his fists. 'I dreamt about that cake last night. You all have to taste it – it's amazing.'

Magdalena lifted the lid of a huge glass dome and began to cut the iced confection.

Lawrence Ridley walked through the door, carrying the last of the bags. 'Hola Magdalena,' he called, and this time it was the cook's face that turned a deep shade of crimson. 'Magdalena, are you all right?'

'Mister Lawrence, you know that your smile makes my heart beat faster than an expressive train. You are far too good-looking for my health.' Magdalena fanned herself and pushed a slice of cake towards Lucas.

Jacinta giggled. She knew exactly how the woman felt.

'Seriously, Mags, don't you think he's getting a bit old these days?' Lucas said, as he plunged his fork into the chocolate treat.

Magdalena waved her hand dismissively. 'Oh, Master Lucas, your father will still be handsome when he is one hundred and I am dead in a box. And you are lucky I let you get away with calling me that. Only you. And maybe your father.'

'This cake is incredible,' Sep said, licking his lips.

'I told you so,' Lucas mumbled with his mouth full. 'I wish you could come and cook for us at school, Magdalena – all the boys would fall in love with you.'

The woman rolled her eyes. 'Now you are being silly. I could not leave the twins – they would starve without me, although I could believe those boys would love me.'

Lucas glanced at the door and spotted his step-mother tiptoeing into the room. Charlotte pressed her finger to her lips.

Lawrence had plonked himself down on a stool at the end of the bench and was about to tuck into a slice of cake. 'I think you'd have to go to war with Charlotte to get Magdalena over to Fayle,' he said, 'and I'm not letting her go anywhere either. My wife is good at a lot of things, but I have to be honest, cooking is definitely not one of her strengths.'

Charlotte crept up behind her husband and

put her hands over his eyes. 'I heard that, Lawrence Ridley,' she said, pouting. 'And you know I'm the first to admit that my culinary skills are somewhat lacking.'

'Oops.' Lawrence took his wife's hands in his and kissed them sheepishly. 'What have you done with the twins?'

Just as he asked, Alice-Miranda and Millie came through the door, with Imogen attached to her cousin's hand and Marcus holding tightly to Millie. The toddlers were both carting the stuffed toys Millie had won under their free arms – but not for long. As soon as they saw their father was home, the shark and the elephant hit the floor and the twins raced over and hugged Lawrence's legs.

'We've been to the pier,' Millie declared, as she and Alice-Miranda hurried over to greet their friends. More cake was cut and the conversation turned to the movie, with the first-time actors talking over the top of one another and firing a hundred questions at Lawrence. The poor man was struggling to keep up.

'I'm afraid I don't know my lines very well yet,' Lawrence admitted. He took a sip of the tea Magdalena had set down in front of him. 'You lot might have to help me tonight. And I can't believe I agreed to sing – although the director might have some concerns once he hears me again.'

'I doubt it, darling,' Charlotte said. 'You've got a fabulous voice. I hope the twins take after you, or else they'll end up sounding like a pair of croaky canaries, seeing as though my singing skills come a close second to my cooking.'

'Oh, Missus Charlotte, your cooking is much better than your singing,' Magdalena piped up. 'I was so scared when I heard you the other day. I thought Missus Goldberg's cat was being strangled! I even went to look for Tinkles in the garden, but then I realised it was just you singing to the babies.' Magdalena laughed so hard that tears began streaming from her eyes and her reaction was contagious.

'At least there's no chance of getting a big head in this family,' Charlotte said, trying to stop the grin that was creeping onto her lips. 'Now, may I have a slice of that delicious chocolate cake that I can guarantee I had absolutely nothing to do with?'

Chapter 6

Tish Crawford sat at the chipped laminex table in the kitchen of the tiny rented condo she shared with her son. She closed the file on a towering pile of bills, having retrieved the most urgent ones for payment, though it was increasingly difficult to work out which utility they could live without. When your child was as talented as Blade, you had to see how far his career could go. If only her parents had recognised her talents at the same age, Tish thought. She could have been an actor or a model instead of marrying a potato farmer in Idaho – not that there was anything wrong with that. She loved her husband – Ray was a good man – but she wasn't going to let her son miss a single opportunity. Fortunately, Ray agreed with her. He'd only taken over the farm because that's what his parents had expected. But now they were gone, he was keen to try his hand at other things. They'd had the place up for sale for months, but the market was stale and there hadn't been a lot of interest.

In the lounge room Blade was flicking through the television channels, wondering why half of them had disappeared. His thoughts turned to his sisters. They were probably feeding the menagerie of animals the family had adopted over the years. There was Phyllis the ginger cat, Weebly the mutt with the stumpy tail, and Charo the chicken that considered itself a lounge singer. There was a sheep called La-La too, which the girls had hand-raised, after it had been abandoned by its mother. Blade didn't really know him because he was a recent addition, but they'd named him after Los Angeles in his honour.

Blade's stomach twisted when he thought about his father and the girls and how much he missed them. He loved acting and knew he was good at it, but Hollywood was hard. He worried about his family and what being apart was doing to them.

Blade got up from the settee and headed into the kitchen. 'Do you think we should go home to be with Dad and the girls?' he asked.

Tish spun around. 'Are you serious, Blade? After everything we've been through to get here?'

'That's not even my real name,' the boy groaned. 'I'm tired, Mum. And I know you can't afford all the singing and acting classes. You haven't had a new pair of shoes since we moved here.' The boy spied a brochure on the table. 'And there is no way I'm taking ballroom dancing lessons!'

'Your father and I are doing this for *you*, Blade. Because you're the one who's got the talent. If you want to go home, then let's do it. Pack your things. We'll start driving tonight. We can be there tomorrow and you can go back to school with all your little friends who are going to end up exactly like their parents – eking out a living for the rest of their lives, never going anywhere, trapped on a roundabout of boring.'

'That's not fair, Mum,' Blade said. 'I miss Dad and the girls, that's all.'

The red rash that always accompanied an outburst began creeping up Tish's neck. 'Do you think I *want* to be away from them? Do you think it doesn't break my heart every time they call and ask me to read them a bedtime story? And you know that the rain has affected the crops; your father is relying on us more than ever to tide things over until we can sell the farm.' Tish slumped down at the kitchen table, with her head in her hands. Next thing the tears would come. It was like a scene from a bad movie except that this was their life, and Blade had seen it far too many times before.

He sat down beside his mum and put an arm around her shoulders. 'I'm sorry. I know how much you've given up for me to have this chance. It's just . . . I miss home.'

'This movie is going to be your big break – I can feel it,' Tish said, pulling a tissue from her pocket. 'But you can't mess it up. Promise me you won't.'

Blade nodded. 'It would have been so much better if I had the lead,' he mumbled. 'I should have got it – I'm way more talented than Sasha. He keeps forgetting his lines and he looks ridiculous in his costume.'

Tish Crawford dabbed at her eyes. Blade was

right, of course. Blade getting the lead would change everything. She could pay off the bills, get a condo close to the studios. It was the first sensible thing she'd heard all day. Now she just had to make it happen.

Chapter 7

Tyger Lombardi drove into the underground parking garage. She switched off the ignition and took a few minutes to carefully pack away her camera. Disappointingly, she hadn't got any more shots of Charlotte Highton-Smith and her twins – who knew you could get fifteen green lights in a row on Santa Monica Boulevard. When Charlotte turned left at Rodeo Drive, Tyger thought it best to head home and not risk another run-in with the police. She hopped out of the car and took her gear with her, riding the lift to her apartment on the fourth floor.

Tyger set her bag down on the couch and wandered into the kitchen, where she flicked on the kettle and pulled a tea bag from the caddy on the bench. She dropped it into her favourite china cup that was miraculously sitting washed on the side of the sink. Tyger couldn't believe her luck this afternoon. Hopefully, no one else had seen Charlotte and the twins down on the pier. It would have been fantastic if Lawrence had made an appearance, but beggars couldn't be choosers. The movie star's wife and children were better than nothing at all.

Just as Tyger was about to sit on the couch with her cup of tea, the door buzzer rang, startling her. 'Darn!' she exclaimed, and grabbed a dishcloth to wipe up the tea she'd spilt onto her jeans. She scraped her long dark hair back into a ponytail as she walked to the intercom by the front door. 'Hello?' she said, peering at the screen.

'Tyger Lombardi?' a gruff voice replied. It belonged to a man she didn't recognise.

'Yes,' she said tentatively.

'You've got something that doesn't belong to

you. I'm giving you five minutes to bring it down here or I'm coming up,' the man growled.

Tyger's mind raced. 'I – I'm not sure what you mean,' she said.

'Oh yes, you do. My boss wants it back. Now!'

Tyger's heart thumped in her chest and she suddenly felt short of breath. She had no idea who this man was or how he knew where she lived, let alone what he was after. The buzzer sounded again, and this time there was an edge to the man's voice.

'I know you've got it, Tyger. If you don't open this door, I'm going to kick it in and then I'm going to come up there and kick in your apartment door too.' The man looked into the camera and, for just a second, Tyger felt as if he were staring right at her. 'Don't think I won't.'

Tyger gulped and stepped back from the monitor, unsure of what to do. She glanced around her messy apartment, searching for an answer, and when she turned back to the screen, the menacing man was gone. With trembling hands, Tyger called her neighbour from across the hall. Anders was a giant Swedish fellow who had come to LA in the hopes of becoming a movie star. So far he'd scored a couple of parts in films as a bodyguard, and when he wasn't auditioning he spent his time working out. He was built like a truck, but underneath his rock-hard exterior was a teddy bear. She'd had to stop herself from laughing when he'd bought himself a tiny shih tzu pup that had quickly become the light of his life. If she told him she thought there was someone roaming the building, she knew he'd check it out for her. And he did.

Anders walked down the fire stairs to the main entrance, but there was no one inside. He took the lift back up and stopped on each floor to be sure. Meanwhile, Tyger rushed around the apartment, trying to tidy up. She hurriedly stuffed things away in cupboards and bags.

'Whoever was down there has gone,' he reported to Tyger through her security-chained door.

'Thanks for checking. It's this pesky guy I went on a date with last month. He won't take no for an answer,' she lied. 'Hey, would you like to join me for dinner tonight? I was about to whip up my famous spaghetti bolognaise.'

That was entirely untrue, but Tyger was sure she had some mince in the freezer and could probably cobble something together. At least she'd washed up that morning and the kitchen wasn't a total disaster.

'It sounds delicious, but I am taking Petra to the puppy park to play with her friends,' Anders said with a grin. 'I promised her this morning and she has been excited all day. But I will take a . . . what do you call it? A raincheck?'

Tyger smiled. 'Raincheck it is.'

If only the strange man at the door *was* a pesky ex-boyfriend, but she had absolutely no idea who he was and what he thought she had that belonged to him. She needed to work that out and sooner rather than later, before someone got hurt.

Chapter 8

The black SUV pulled up at the gate as the driver lowered the heavily tinted window. Spanning the width of the driveway above them was a huge sign for Goldberg Studios with the famous clapperboard icon. The jovial guard waved as the car drove through the gates and onto the studio lot. Bob negotiated his way through a maze of streets before they stopped outside a two-storey office building. Beside it was an enormous shed that resembled an aircraft hangar. Lawrence and the children piled out of the car and were met by a young woman who was wearing a headset and clutching a clipboard.

'Kids, this is Emmy. Her official title is First Assistant Director, but, really, I think they should call her the busiest person on the lot. She will be looking after you, making sure that you're where you need to be when you need to be there,' Lawrence said. 'And she's fierce –' he winked and put his hand up to shield his mouth – 'so don't mess with her.'

Emmy pretended to swat the famous actor with her clipboard. 'I'm only fierce with people who aren't where they're supposed to be when they're meant to be there,' she protested, feigning insult, then turned to the children and grinned. 'I'm so excited to meet you all. This is going to be a fun shoot. Come on, I'll show you around.'

The group followed Emmy inside the building, which wasn't at all what they had expected. Almost as soon as they'd walked through the door, a woman charged towards them, practically bowing as she asked Lawrence if he wanted anything – tea, coffee, chai latte, activated almonds, whatever his heart desired. Lucas and the children suppressed smirks as the woman continued her long list of offerings. Lawrence politely declined, but the eager assistant was having none of it and was convinced that, according to information she had obtained, Lawrence was due a strongly brewed white tea served in a china cup at this time of the morning. She promptly dashed off to procure it.

'Whoa, what is this place?' Millie breathed, gazing around the giant structure.

The entire left half of the inside comprised a wide main street with houses and shops lining either side. There were cactus plants, fully grown trees and mounds and mounds of dirt. It looked as if a Wild West town had been transplanted from the desert. The opposite end of the vast building played host to various cameras and other technical equipment as well as a grand piano in the far corner.

'Welcome to sound stage seven,' Emmy said proudly. 'Pretty impressive, huh?'

'I can't believe someone built all of this just for a movie,' Jacinta said in amazement. She did a full three-hundred-and-sixty-degree twirl on the spot, trying to take it all in.

'Wait until tomorrow, when we start shooting – it will look even better,' Emmy promised.

Two huge doors peeled back on the other side of the building and the beeping of a reversing truck filled the space. The vehicle dumped a load of red dirt in the middle of the Wild West street and a group of workmen started spreading it around.

'Where would you like these rocks?' a man called out to the fellow in charge. A small excavator began lifting giant stones off the back of the flatbed as another chap raced over to orchestrate their placement. The site was busier than an ants' nest.

Lawrence sat down on a chair with his name printed across the back of it and flipped open the script he was carrying. The insistent woman returned with some tea and a plate of Lawrence's favourite biscuits for good measure. While he ran through his lines, the children continued their explorations.

'Hey, there's Caprice and Mr Lipp,' Millie said, pointing to the pair standing next to the piano. No one was going to miss Mr Lipp today, dressed as he was in a bright green suit with a peacock-blue cravat and matching polka-dotted handkerchief protruding from his breast pocket. A woman wearing a startling red dress with a bold slash of lipstick and the most extraordinary pile of white-blonde curls atop her head was tinkling the ivories and barking orders at Mr Lipp, who was frantically scribbling notes on the scoresheet. Neither of them seemed remotely interested in Caprice, who had her arms folded tightly in front of her. The girl's demeanour softened with relief as she caught sight of the other children.

'Thank goodness you're here,' she said, after slipping away to join them. 'I am *so* bored. Hairy and Griz have been faffing about with the music all morning and I'm yet to sing a note. My call sheet said I had to be here at the crack of dawn for rehearsals, but I could have come with you guys after all,' she grumbled. 'Mummy left straight away to see about her television special, so I've been completely alone.'

Caprice and her mother had arrived at Lawrence and Charlotte's Beverly Hills mansion late last evening. By that time, the rest of the children had gone to bed.

'How frustrating. You must be tired too, having got in so late,' Alice-Miranda sympathised.

'I'm exhausted and I hardly slept – I wish we were in the main house. Charlotte has obviously put the cast-off mattresses with lumps in them in the guesthouse,' Caprice complained.

Lucas caught Sep's eye and shook his head. Millie fought hard to still her tongue.

'Have you met any of the other actors?' Sloane asked.

Caprice scoffed. 'If you could call them that. Yesterday, I met Sasha, whose grandfather owns the studio, and Sophie, who plays the role of my little sister – she's quite sweet – and there was a boy named Blade.'

'Is he pretty sharp?' Millie asked with a snort.

Caprice rolled her eyes. 'You're so lame.'

'At least I'm not rude and ungrateful,' Millie spat back, as Alice-Miranda glided in and steered the group towards Lawrence, who was talking to himself and sipping the tea he hadn't wanted.

Caprice spotted Sophie arriving and brought her over to meet everyone. Millie commented that Sophie looked a lot like Alice-Miranda, and the girl was beginning to explain how she had to wear a blonde wig for her part so she could pass as Caprice's sister when Emmy gathered the group together.

'Okay, kids. First up, I'd like to welcome you all to Goldberg Studios. I really hope that you're going to have an awesome time and, please, if there is anything you need, just ask. I'm here to look after you.' Emmy glanced at her watch and wondered if she should give Tish Crawford and Aviva Goldberg a ring. They were meant to be here by now. Before she could reach for the phone, the doors opened and Blade and his mother walked into the building, followed by Sasha and Aviva.

'Sorry we're late. There was a pile-up on the freeway and we had to go the long way around,' Tish explained.

'It was a disaster,' Aviva whined.

Alice-Miranda's eyes widened in concern. 'Were you involved in the accident?'

Aviva Goldberg shook her head. 'If only to be put out of our misery! We're here now and Sasha is so excited – aren't you, my booboola?' Aviva reached out and pinched her son's cheeks, which were now redder than Millie's hair.

'He doesn't look excited to me,' Millie whispered to Alice-Miranda. 'I think he looks mortified.'

'Poor boy is probably embarrassed walking into such a big group,' Alice-Miranda replied. 'Perhaps we're a bit overwhelming.' Although Alice-Miranda did think maybe it was due to the fact that Mrs Goldberg was somewhat larger than life.

Emmy introduced Blade and Sasha and told the children they could all get to know each other better at morning tea.

'Where's Venetia?' Aviva asked, looking around. She was hoping that the woman might take them to another delightful eatery.

'I'm afraid she's working,' Emmy said. 'But she did tell me about a fabulous new cafe on Selma Avenue.' Emmy produced a piece of paper from her pocket and handed it over. Having seen Aviva's enthusiasm yesterday, she'd asked Venetia for some tips that would guarantee moving the woman offsite.

'Are you up for it, Tish?' Aviva asked.

Blade's mother nodded. 'Of course. I couldn't think of anything I'd rather do.' After spending much of the previous day with Aviva, Tish was now lying through her teeth, but she wanted to know more about Sasha and his acting ambitions and how easy it might be to get rid of the kid.

'Let's get going then. I think morning tea first, then lunch at Luigi's and perhaps we could squeeze in a little shopping?' Aviva prattled, sashaying towards the exit. 'My treat.'

'Your mother is lovely,' Alice-Miranda whispered to Sasha.

'She's okay,' the boy said, twisting his fingers nervously. 'If you don't mind being embarrassed twenty times a day.'

Millie smiled at him. 'Isn't that what parents are for? My dad is always saying things that make me cringe, but he's kind of funny too except when he's telling dodgy dad jokes. I'll give you an example: You'd better keep your eyes open tomorrow.'

Sasha shrugged.

'Because you won't see anything if you don't.' Millie grinned. 'He likes to try that one on all my friends.'

Sasha chortled. 'You're right. That is bad.'

'It must be pretty cool that your family owns the studio, though,' Millie said.

'I guess,' Sasha replied quietly. 'Lots of kids are super nice to me until they get to come out here and then they don't usually hang around. Unless it's my birthday. Mum throws the best parties.'

Alice-Miranda and Millie looked at each other and frowned. Alice-Miranda hated the idea that the boy was so lonely. She resolved to do everything she could to make him feel welcome in their group. Little did she know that Millie was thinking the exact same thing.

Emmy tapped her pen on her clipboard as the piano reached a crescendo in the background. 'Right then, shall we get started?'

Chapter 9

Harold Lipp distributed a pile of song sheets while chairs were located for the children to sit on. 'Now,' he began, 'I know we've been rehearsing back at home, but Frau Furtwangler is in charge from this point and I expect you to listen carefully to what she has to say.'

'Frau Furtwangler?' Sloane giggled. 'Who's that?'

Before there was time for the titters to continue, the woman in the red dress stood up from the piano seat and turned around. 'I am Frau Furtwangler,' she said in a strong German accent. She cast her eyes over the children. 'I am in charge and you vill do vot I say or I vill squash you like a bug beneath my foot – and my foot is extra large.' She pointed at a patent red peeptoe that in all fairness did seem bigger than that of the average woman.

The children gulped.

'Ve are not here for fun,' the woman continued. 'If you accepted this role because you thought you were going to be playing namby-pamby-oopsy-la-la – a nice little singsong in a movie – then you are sadly mistaken. My music is perfection and I do NOT tolerate idiots or mistakes. So take your pick – are you an idiot or are you a mistake? No doubt you vill show to me that you are both.' Frau Furtwangler turned to Mr Lipp. 'Shall ve begin?'

The man nodded eagerly. 'Oh yes, of course. Children, please stand.'

Grizelda Furtwangler stretched her arms above her head before sitting down and kicking off her shoes. She then slowly cracked her knuckles one by one. The children flinched at the sound. After several minutes passed, the frau placed her fingers on the keys and began to play a long introduction. 'Make sure that you get the first note correct as it is a tricky one on the down beat,' she bellowed.

Harold Lipp exhaled as he counted under his breath. He raised his hand into the air and the children commenced singing. But instead of playing a melodious tune, Frau Furtwangler bashed her hands against the keys, creating an almighty cacophony.

'No, no, no, no, no!' she shouted. 'Mr Lipp, you are TOO early. Are you an idiot also? We must start again. From the top!'

The children looked at their teacher, whose breathing had quickened along with everyone else's pulses.

'I'm sorry,' he grovelled, beads of sweat springing to his temples. 'I'll get it right this time.'

They almost made it to the end before the woman threw her hands into the air for a second time.

'Stop, stop! Mr Lipp, is there blood here?' Grizelda demanded, signalling to her right ear.

Harold Lipp leaned in to take a peek. 'I . . . I don't think so,' he stammered. He pulled his polka-dotted handkerchief from his breast pocket and mopped at his brow.

'Vell, I am surprised because –' Frau Furtwangler spun around on her piano stool and pointed – 'you and you and you all sang notes that should have made my ears *bleed*.'

Sloane, Millie and Lucas shrunk down in their seats.

'I didn't think we were that bad,' Lucas grumbled, barely moving his lips.

The children took a nervous breath and started again. This time, much to everyone's relief, they made it to the end without any further upsets.

'Well done, everyone,' Mr Lipp praised the group. He imagined he felt something akin to that of an expectant mother after giving birth to a twelve-pound baby.

Frau Furtwangler glared at him and gave a brusque tsk-tsk. 'Too much praise too soon,' she remonstrated, rolling her shoulders and causing the sequins on her dress to crunch. 'Now, get me some tea. I am parched and I need a back rub.'

Millie wrinkled her nose and Alice-Miranda giggled behind her hand.

Harold Lipp stood frozen to the spot, trying to work out which of the frau's requests he should attend to first. He flexed his fingers and reached out to begin the massage when she turned on him.

'Get my tea!' she fumed. 'My masseuse is on her vay.'

Harold Lipp retreated and raced off in search of a brew. The woman was impossible, but he still couldn't believe how fortunate he was to be working with such a genius.

The children were given a recess break to grab a drink and a quick bite to eat. Under their musical director's orders, they were only to drink tepid tea or warm water with lemon and honey, which no one seemed particularly excited by. At least the food was more in keeping with the children's tastes. In fact, the food was incredible. There were chocolate-chip biscuits and macarons, red velvet cupcakes, fruit platters, bowls of nuts and chips, and enough sandwiches to fill at least fifty school lunch boxes.

Frau Furtwangler drank her tea while having her shoulders massaged by a woman in a white jumpsuit and still managing to play the piano at the same time. She barked orders at Mr Lipp, who jotted down changes to the score and jiggled like a bobble-head dog on a car dashboard.

'Is she always so bossy?' Sloane asked Emmy, who was busy handing out cupcakes and sandwiches.

Emmy smiled knowingly. 'Grizelda Furtwangler has a reputation for being a bit of a tough cookie, but she is one of the best musical directors in Hollywood. The results will be worth it, just you wait and see.'

Sloane grimaced. 'A bit tough? I'd hate to see her when she's really wound up.'

'I think it's wonderful Frau Furtwangler is so intent on getting the very best out of us,' Alice-Miranda commented. 'And have you seen the way Mr Lipp looks at her? He's completely in awe.'

Millie was part way through devouring the most delicious sandwich she'd ever tasted. 'I thought we'd be in a dark studio somewhere recording the music,' the girl said, apparently practising her ventriloquism skills and trying not to spray anyone with her food. 'Like when you see bands recording on television.' She gobbled the last bite and reached for another triangle.

'That's what usually happens, but Grizelda favours the acoustics in here, so we're having a whole lot of equipment moved in for the orchestra this afternoon,' Emmy explained. 'Don't take anything she says to heart. I can assure you, she treats everyone with the same level of contempt.'

'Soloists,' Frau Furtwangler roared. 'I need to hear you and you had better be good or I vill be screaming my hair out.'

Mr Lipp looked at Caprice and Sasha. 'I hope you've both brought your A-game this morning, children.'

Caprice tossed her copper curls over her shoulder and fluttered her eyelashes. Sasha shrugged and stuffed the last of the iced doughnut he was eating into his mouth.

'Ve vill start from the fourth bar in,' Grizelda declared, and launched into the music, her fingers dancing up and down the keys.

Caprice was on pitch from the first note. She sang the verse perfectly before the rest of the children joined in for the chorus. Blade felt a shiver run down his spine. He tried not to stare at the girl with the angelic voice, but it was as if she'd cast a spell on him. Then it was Sasha's turn. His voice trembled and was barely audible. Mr Lipp's arms were flapping about as he urged the boy to sing louder. When Sasha finally increased the volume, the sound wasn't quite what anyone had expected.

Grizelda stopped playing and glared at the lad. 'Vot is that you are doing?'

'Um . . . singing?' the boy offered.

Grizelda breathed deeply, her nostrils flaring ever so slightly. 'If that vas singing then I am currently doing lengths of an Olympic pool, on the back of a dolphin who is varing a tutu and eating cheese puffs!'

'I . . . I can do better,' Sasha stammered. His ears were now pinker than his cheeks.

'Oh, you had better do better. Or you vill be gone,' she growled. 'I can tell you now that there are other boys in this group who I could replace you vith.'

'You can do it,' Alice-Miranda mouthed to him.

But Sasha looked as if he were about to throw up. He nodded unconvincingly, then clutched at his stomach and ran across the sound stage towards the bathroom.

'I'll go after him,' Emmy said, a look of grave concern etched into her features. The last thing she needed was a blow-up between Aviva Goldberg and Frau Furtwangler.

Blade watched on with delight. 'I know his part,' he volunteered, seizing his chance. 'I auditioned for it.'

'Vell, let's see vot you can do then,' the woman said, resuming her place at the keys and ordering him to sing.

Chapter 10

Abe Goldberg sat opposite his son, not quite believing what he'd just heard. In his grey three-piece suit and perfectly coiffed silver hair, the man was a picture of calm elegance, but on the inside he was fuming. Although there was a strong facial resemblance between the pair, Abe was tall and broad-shouldered while his son had developed a huge gut, no doubt aided by the amount of food his wife insisted on serving up each night. There was a knock on the door and Abe's assistant entered with a tray of tea and biscuits.

'Thank you, Carol,' he said, as she placed it on the side of the desk and made her retreat. He still managed a smile for her, despite the storm that was brewing. His grin instantly melted into a frown as he turned back to his son. 'You said that Enzo was on board. He was going to be here today – no matter what,' Abe challenged.

Eli shrugged. 'He was supposed to wrap last week, but who knew that Romania was about to get the worst rain they'd had in fifty years. So, unless you want to further delay filming, I don't see that we have any option but to hand it to someone else.'

'And who exactly do you have in mind?' Abe lifted his teacup to his lips and took a sip.

'A new guy – Andreas King. He's done some interesting indie stuff and I think he's ready for the big time,' Eli replied. He drummed the fingers on his right hand impatiently against his thigh. This was never going to be a fun conversation and he dearly wanted to get out of there as quickly as he could.

'Never heard of him.' Abe put his cup down with a sharp chink. 'If this is your idea of a joke, then I don't much like your sense of humour. You know how important this project is to me and you're giving it to some kid who's wet behind the ears?'

Eli pushed back against his chair. 'Well, it's too late now because he signed his contract this morning. We don't have time to find anyone else.'

Abe could feel his pulse racing and the vein near his temple was beginning to throb. He had to calm down or Eli would be calling his mother and telling her that Abe was in danger of another turn. He wasn't about to allow that to happen. While there was still breath in his body, he would be in charge of this studio. 'Why wasn't I consulted first?' he pressed.

'Timing, Dad, and the budget is tight on this one. All the kids are on set today and Lawrence and Alexa have arrived too. You know those kids only have a couple of weeks at most.'

Unfortunately, his son was right on both counts. The board hadn't been thrilled about the film in the first place and the last thing he needed was twitchy investors. They couldn't afford to wait for Enzo and he wanted the movie out for the holidays. It had to be in the mix for next year's award season too. He owed her memory that much.

Chapter 11

Boomer stretched his way up from the beaten beanbag that sat in front of the fireplace and wandered over to join his mistress.

'What is it, Boom?' Aislin asked.

The faithful bloodhound glanced up at her with the saddest brown eyes she'd ever known. When he'd come to her as a puppy she couldn't believe there was another creature on the earth who looked more miserable than she did, but he'd been a true blessing these past ten years. God willing, she'd shuffle off before him; the thought of losing another one was almost more than she could bear. The dog howled and stared in the direction of the porch.

Aislin struggled out of the lounge chair. It was covered in colourful crocheted throws, hiding the fact that it, like every other stick of furniture in the place, had seen better days. She walked to the front window and pulled back the net curtains. In the distance, she could see the dust pluming behind the pick-up truck like a dragon's tail. It would bring her another month of supplies, although how much longer he'd need to come was debatable. Garber was reliable, if nothing else. That man wouldn't be stopped by flood or fire or even a pesky hip that the doctor kept telling him he needed to replace.

Aislin opened and closed the fingers of her left hand. They ached especially bad today and the crocheting hadn't helped. Doc had said it was best to keep her hands moving to slow down the arthritis that had already buckled the end of her left pinky into a crook. Fortunately, the condition only affected her hands and otherwise she'd kept herself fit with walking. There were days she and Boomer set off early in the morning and returned at dusk, having covered many miles without coming upon another living soul. The silence would have driven most folks crazy, but Aislin loved the feeling of being so small in a place where the sky stretched on for eternity.

She watched as the dust trail snaked its way up from the road, zigzagging left and right before it reached the front of the house and the vehicle was enveloped in a rust-coloured cloud.

'Morning, Miss Devine,' Garber said, as he limped around to the back of the truck. 'I got you some corned beef, and that mustard you were after finally came in. There's a big ol' crate of pumpkins too – you'll be making pies and soup till the next time I get up here. And, ma'am, I got a box of books so large you'll be dreamin' stories in your sleep.'

'Hmph. I'll probably be dead the next time you come,' she said.

Garber unloaded the first box from the tray and walked into the house. 'What's got you so cheery today?' he asked.

'I'm being realistic, is all,' Aislin replied. She watched him walk back and forth from the kitchen, where he piled the boxes. When he'd finished unloading the last of them, he began unpacking everything and putting the items away. 'Coffee?' she asked, already knowing the answer.

'Thank you, ma'am.'

With a tired grunt, Boomer moseyed down the front steps and out into the yard, sniffing this and that.

'I hear they'll be shooting a film 'bout twenty miles this side of the West Rim next week,' Garber said. He took off his hat and scratched his head. 'The biggest names in Hollywood are coming. Lawrence Ridley and Alexa Mills, so my sources tell me. I'm gonna get me their autographs.'

'Well, you enjoy yourself, Garb. Just don't come bothering me. I don't want to have anything to do with anyone.'

Garber surely knew that. Miss Devine had lived out there for longer than he could remember. He'd been delivering her groceries for longer than that, and in all those years he couldn't recall one single person being at that house except her and a dog. Always a bloodhound; over the years there had been Sadie then Duke then Bruiser and now Boomer. She was a woman who knew her mind – somehow grew vegetables in a place where nothing much grew. Somehow managed to keep chickens when they should have been coyote supper. Miss Devine was about as lovely a person as you'd ever meet, and in all the time he'd been coming here he'd done his best to get to know her, but she wasn't one for personal conversations. He reckoned Miss Devine must have been a real beauty when she was young, before whatever it was that had happened to her.

He downed the last drop of his coffee and put his cup in the sink. 'Thank you very much for that, ma'am. I'll be seeing you the first of next month.' He nodded firmly to let her know that was not negotiable.

Aislin retrieved an old tin from the top of the cupboard and took out a chequebook. She studied the amount on the invoice and then wrote out a cheque to Garber Sheedy. Her handwriting was getting more like spidery scrawl with each passing month. Aislin handed him the cheque. 'There you are, Garb. You take care of that hip.'

The pair walked outside.

'You take care too, Miss Devine.' Garber grinned a yellowed smile as he slipped behind the wheel.

'Come on back here, Boomer, you silly old dog,' she called, and the bloodhound did exactly as he was bid.

Chapter 12

Millie's stomach grumbled for what felt like the hundredth time. It was after one o'clock and the children were yet to eat lunch. Frau Furtwangler had insisted they sing through the score twice and then once more for good measure. Even though Sasha had returned from the bathroom looking rather pasty, it didn't seem to worry the musical director that Blade was still singing the boy's part. Sasha didn't seem to mind either. In fact, he hoped that no one else would notice.

'That's a wrap up for now,' Grizelda said, ending the piece with a flourish. 'This afternoon ve vill rehearse vith the orchestra.'

'She's a slavedriver,' Jacinta griped, thankfully out of earshot of the woman.

Sep grinned. 'I was half expecting her to start cracking a whip for real.'

'Is there anything else I can do for you, Frau Furtwangler?' Mr Lipp asked eagerly.

'Get out of my vay,' the woman said, standing up. She turned to Emmy. 'I presume that my bungalow is prepared?'

Emmy nodded. She had tripled-checked this morning that the bungalow Frau Furtwangler con-sidered her own personal home away from home had been stocked with German sausage, schnitzel, sauerkraut and apple strudel. There was also a chilled bottle of Moselle from her favourite vineyard, four green apples and exactly thirty-one white grapes. The bungalow, one of ten on the lot, was comprised of a bedroom, en-suite bathroom, lounge area and a state-of-the-art kitchen. Emmy often thought she'd love to live in one of them, given how much time she spent at work, but, no, they were reserved for the big stars and directors. While they were all lovely, bungalow number one was by far the most coveted. Frau Furtwangler had it written into her contract that, whenever she was on set, it was hers.

'I vill eat in forty-five minutes and do not forget that I detest overcooked sausages. It is not good for my indigestion,' Frau Furtwangler reminded her. The woman slid back into her heels and strode out of the building.

'Or her disposition,' Emmy mumbled to herself. The young woman paused to check that Frau Furtwangler hadn't returned lest she be told off for praising the children unduly. 'Well done, everyone,' she said quietly. 'This score is going to sound incredible.'

'Yes, I can only agree,' Mr Lipp said. 'But I could murder a cup of tea and a sandwich. Actually, some sausages would have been nice.' He'd been secretly hoping that Frau Furtwangler might invite him to join her for lunch.

The group followed Emmy out of the building and across the street to what looked like another movie set. It seemed to go on as far as the eye could see and spanned both sides of the road.

'This is New York in the 1950s for now,' she explained, as the children tripped along the street lined with brownstone buildings. 'But we can pretty much adapt it to be New York during any period.'

Millie ran her hand over one of the facades, marvelling at how real it looked, right down to the fine cracks in the masonry. She realised she'd fallen behind the others, and ran to catch up. 'Are the bricks and everything genuine?' she asked.

Sloane skipped over to a window and peered through it. 'Is there anything behind these fronts?' she asked, squinting into the darkness.

Emmy smiled and shook her head. 'I'm afraid not. The guys in post-production can transform a single-storey facade into a building that's a hundred storeys high onscreen through the magic of CGI,' she said, leading them over to a big carport with a shiny red Cadillac convertible parked beside a stereo speaker.

'So, Hollywood really is all smoke and mirrors,' Millie said. After the research she'd undertaken before their trip, she'd known to expect as much, but a tiny part of her couldn't help feeling a little disappointed.

'It's amazing, isn't it?' Alice-Miranda said. 'Computer-generated imagery has come such a long way. I was watching an old monster movie with Daddy the other night and it was so obvious the creature was just a toy suspended on strings. These days, though, it's almost impossible to tell what's real and what's not.'

'Where are we going?' Blade asked. They had stopped in front of what appeared to be an old American diner.

'You'll see.' Emmy grinned and pushed open the door.

'Whoa!' Millie gasped, her eyes on stalks. 'But I thought you said the whole street was fake.'

'Everything except for Patty's,' Emmy said with a twinkle in her eye. 'We've got about an hour for lunch, so make sure you eat up and then we'll have a quick look around before we head back to the sound stage.'

Millie plonked herself down in the first booth and grabbed the menu from the middle of the table. 'Burgers!' she exclaimed. 'They have burgers and curly fries and pizza too.' The child was almost drooling at the thought of it all.

'I haven't had a hot dog in ages,' Lucas said, licking his lips.

After settling on what to order, the children made their way up to the counter. Three women dressed in outfits that matched the diner's red-and-white decor beamed at the children as they made their requests.

'Is it okay if I have a little bit of everything?' Sep asked.

A woman with dark frizzy hair, and whose badge revealed her name was Layla, smiled at the boy. 'With manners as lovely as yours, young man, I'd say you can have one of everything and then come back for seconds.'

It didn't take long before each child had been served. Alice-Miranda and Millie slid into a booth with Sloane, while Jacinta and Lucas were seated with Sep, Blade and Sophie.

Caprice walked back to the tables, casting around for somewhere to sit.

'Would you like to join us?' Alice-Miranda asked. 'There's plenty of room.'

Even Millie didn't object, which was a sure sign of some progress in their relationship.

'Thanks,' Caprice said, and squeezed in next to Sloane.

Millie noticed that Sasha was alone in a booth right at the very end. She stood up and made her way over to the boy. 'Are you feeling better?' she asked.

He looked up from his plate, which contained a small serving of salad and a tiny piece of chicken.

'Yeah, I'm fine,' he said, his cheeks flushing a bright pink.

'Do you want to come and sit with us?' Millie asked. 'You shouldn't eat on your own. You're making us look mean and I can assure you we're not – well, I can't speak for Caprice.'

Sasha's cheeks darkened. 'She's really talented,' he said softly. 'I don't think I've ever heard a voice as beautiful as hers.'

'True,' Millie said. She kicked herself. 'I shouldn't have said that about Caprice. That made me sound like the mean one. It's just that she's always been tricky, but she's a lot nicer now. Come on, let's stop by the buffet on the way – you need to eat more than that if you're going to survive the afternoon with Grizzie.'

'I'm still not feeling great,' the boy protested.

'You need to keep up your strength,' Millie insisted, and took the boy's plate.

A minute or so later Sasha was seated with his new friends. Blade looked over, wondering how that had happened. The kid was a total loser and now he was sitting with Caprice and everyone was talking to him as though he was okay. It should have been him there, not Sasha. Tomorrow he'd make sure that it was.

Chapter 13

After the children finished their lunch, they boarded a fancy black minibus and drove through the back lot while Emmy pointed out various famous film sets, including a beach scene and a crashed jumbo jet. Convoys of trolley cars containing members of the general public followed a well-worn route, with guides commentating their tours. On a plateau above the back lot sat the Goldberg Studios theme park complete with rides, shows and everything else an amusement park had to offer.

'Will we get to go up there this week?' Sep asked as the bus drove past the set of a popular television show.

'That depends on how fast we get through the filming, but I hope so,' Emmy replied. 'Oh, on your left you'll see the props department and the wardrobe is next door. We'll be heading there for final fittings after our next session.'

The bus turned a corner and pulled up outside the sound stage where they had spent the morning. The children alighted and headed inside. A fellow with wavy brown hair and thick-rimmed tortoise-shell glasses greeted them warmly.

'Hi kids, my name is Wade Riley and I'm your script coach,' he said, then called their names and handed them each a labelled folder.

Everyone's script was marked up for their character. They mostly had scant lines, given that the children were playing young versions of the adult cast at the very beginning of the movie. It was really only Caprice and Sasha who had a lot to remember, although Blade probably had the best lines overall because his character was the cheekiest member of an outlaw gang. Some of Sophie's were funny too, being the naughty little sister.

'Please take a seat. We're going to do a read-through of scene five, then hopefully our director will be here and he can run you through the actions,' Wade explained. 'Before we start, though, this is Hannah, your dialect coach. I trust that everyone has been practising their accents, but if you're having trouble, Hannah is your gal. I think she could train a monkey to speak with a hundred different dialects.'

The man motioned towards a slender woman with glossy chestnut hair tied into a low ponytail. She had a blunt fringe that hovered just above her very intense blue eyes. 'Hi everyone,' she said, giving them a friendly wave. 'I'm here if you need me, and please don't get upset if I stop you at any time. We have to get this right – the less time we're on set, the better. That's what Mr Goldberg always says.'

She looked over at Sasha and winked. The boy gave a wry grin. He'd known Hannah since he was tiny. She was his private speech and drama teacher and he was glad she was working on this film. It made him feel a little more confident that he might at least pull off the speaking parts.

'All right, everyone, we're starting at the top of page seventeen with young Nellie. You can stand up if you'll feel more comfortable, Caprice,' Wade offered. 'And it's probably a good idea for all of you to read from the script at this stage.'

Caprice placed the pages down beside her and got to her feet. 'That won't be necessary. I know it off by heart,' she said, flicking her copper tresses over her shoulder.

Sasha gulped. He'd practised his part almost a hundred times but suddenly couldn't even conjure the first line.

'Okay then, when you're ready,' Wade said.

Caprice began and, not surprisingly, her accent was flawless and she breezed through. When it was his turn, Sasha stumbled over several of his lines and at one point looked at Hannah in panic. She nodded a silent encouragement and he managed the rest of his part with only a couple of minor mistakes. Blade had a few lines too, which he rattled off perfectly without consulting the script once.

They then moved on to the more minor roles and all was well until it was Sloane's turn. How the girl could completely mangle less than a dozen words was anyone's guess.

Wade cleared his throat. 'All right, we might just hold it there for a moment,' he said, trying to disguise his horror.

'Did I do something wrong?' Sloane asked, her forehead puckering.

'Are you serious, Sloane? What was that voice and that terrible accent?' Sep shook his head, embarrassed that they were related. 'You sounded like a Russian pirate who'd spent a lot of time in China and was possibly living with some French tourists.'

The rest of the cast giggled.

Sloane glared at him, then spun around to the others. 'It wasn't that bad, was it?' she asked.

'Yeah, it was,' Millie said.

'Why don't you and I go and work on it?' Hannah suggested, getting to her feet.

Sloane pursed her lips. 'Okay,' she said grudgingly. 'I really thought it sounded fine, though.'

'We'll go again from the beginning of the scene,' Wade advised.

The children quickly turned their pages back to the start. As Caprice cleared her throat, an external door opened, casting a long sliver of light into the building. Lawrence Ridley walked onto the set with a woman who Alice-Miranda immediately recognised as one of her favourite actors, Alexa Mills. Uncle Lawrence had said she had been cast as Nellie, the leading lady in the film. The children nudged each other as they realised who it was that had just come in. The famous actors were followed by Eli Goldberg, who resembled an immaculately dressed bowling pin, and a young chap with a mop of brown curls and a backpack slung over one shoulder.

Sasha Goldberg looked at the four of them and seemed to shrink into himself.

'Hello Mr Goldberg,' Wade said. 'The kids are doing really well. We're ready to start as soon as Mr Rossi arrives.'

'He's not coming,' Eli Goldberg said, waving his hand dismissively.

The children looked at one another in alarm.

'Aren't we making the film any more?' Sasha asked the question that everyone else was thinking, although he doubted they were feeling the potential relief he was.

'If only it were so easy to get your grandfather to abandon his pet project,' Eli said with a scornful laugh. 'Mr Rossi has been delayed on another movie, so I'd like to introduce you to our new director, Andreas King.'

The children glanced around the set and then back at Eli.

'Where is he?' Lucas asked.

'This,' Eli said, pointing at the fellow with the curls beside him, 'is Andreas.'

'He looks like the work-experience kid,' Millie whispered to Jacinta, who laughed behind her hand.

'I thought he was the best boy,' Blade breathed.

'What's that?' Sep asked.

'I'll explain later,' Blade replied.

Eli nudged the new director. 'Are you going to say hello or what?'

'Oh, sure. Hi guys. Looking forward to working with you,' Andreas said.

Alice-Miranda stood up from her seat and walked over to shake the fellow's hand, introducing herself in the usual way. 'It's a pleasure to meet you, Mr King,' she said.

'And you too, Alice-Matilda,' he replied. 'Is there somewhere I can get a cola? I'm parched.'

'I'll get you one,' Emmy said, and scurried away.

'I know Andreas is keen to get started, so I'll leave you all to it,' Eli Goldberg said, then leaned over and whispered in the young man's ear.

Andreas nodded and grinned like a Cheshire cat. 'You won't regret this, sir,' he said, shaking Eli's hand.

Emmy dashed back to the group. 'Here's your

cola, Mr King,' she puffed, handing the man the bottle.

He studied the label, his lip curling. 'Do you have anything organic?'

Millie rolled her eyes. 'Who's ever heard of organic cola?'

Alice-Miranda shrugged. 'I suppose if you could get that anywhere it would be in Hollywood.'

'I'll see what I can do.' Emmy took the bottle back and hurried away.

'Would you like to hear the children run through their lines before we do a full rehearsal on stage?' Wade asked.

'I guess,' Andreas said. He looked around at the crew that had been steadily assembling over the past hour. The sound stage was now fully rigged with lights and cameras, booms and everything else required to make a movie and there were men and women crawling all over the place. There were still a few areas of the set under construction, but they were on the other side of the vast building.

Wade wondered at Andreas's enthusiasm. He would have thought that, given this was his big break, he'd have been raring to go, but perhaps he needed a little time to familiarise himself with the project first. It was a lot to expect of someone to take over at the last minute.

By now Sloane and Hannah had returned to the group.

'Excuse me, Wade, could I introduce Miss Mills to the children before you resume the rehearsal?' Lawrence asked.

'Yes, of course,' Wade said. 'Sorry about that. I'll introduce you both. Kids, this is Lawrence Ridley and Alexa Mills. You'll be sharing the screen with them and I don't think you could be in better hands.'

The children waved and Sep began a round of applause.

'Alexa is so beautiful,' Sloane gasped, much to the chagrin of the rest of the cast, who giggled loudly.

'You're very sweet, but I can tell you that this,' Alexa said, pointing to her face, 'is the very fortunate product of some good genes and hours in hair and make-up.'

Sloane didn't believe that for a second – well, except the part about having good genes. The woman's hair was like silk and she didn't seem to be wearing any make-up at all.

Wade checked his watch and tapped his folder. He was anxious to get a move on as Emmy had just informed him of how much more the children were supposed to get through before the end of the day. A full rehearsal with Frau Furtwangler and the orchestra sounded exhausting to him. 'Let's take it from the beginning of scene five.'

The children delivered their lines perfectly, and the transformation of Sloane's accent was nothing short of a miracle. By the time they reached the end, Lawrence and Alexa clapped loudly, cheering 'bravo' and telling the children how fantastic they were.

'What did you think, Mr King?' Wade asked.

Andreas blinked at him, then pulled two earphones from under his brown curls. 'Sorry, I missed all that. I was catching up on some music.'

Wade gave the man a quizzical look. 'Would you like us to read through the scene again?'

'Yeah, sure,' Andreas said, flashing him a smile.

Alice-Miranda could hear tinny sounds emanating from the earbuds that were now trailing the man's waist. She was trying to work out which song he'd been playing. There was something very familiar about the tune, but not because it was part of the film. The music stopped and Alice-Miranda heard a voice. The director hadn't been listening to the film score at all. It was the radio and it sounded like the Top 40 countdown.

'Okay, kids, let's see if you can do an even better job than the last time,' Wade said, and turned around to make sure that Andreas was listening. 'You ready?' he asked.

'Yeah, sure,' Andreas replied, before burying his head in the folder he was holding.

Alice-Miranda hoped that this time he was actually following the script.

Chapter 14

'So, how did you enjoy your first day on set, kids?' Charlotte Highton-Smith asked, as the family and friends gathered around the dining table. Magdalena had just served up a tantalising chicken dish that had everyone's nostrils twitching with delight.

'The catering was amazing,' Millie fizzed. 'I've never seen so many varieties of nuts in one place and who knew that almonds could be active?'

'I think you mean "activated", Millie,' Venetia laughed. 'But don't ask me what the difference between them and the regular variety is.' The woman ate a piece of chicken and almost melted. She wondered about the elusive ingredient she couldn't quite put her finger on.

'We met Alexa Mills and she's drop-dead gorgeous,' Lucas said. He paused, feeling the brunt of Jacinta's glare, then quickly added, 'In a very average, normal, almost dreary kind of way.'

'Everyone treats Lawrence like he's a god,' Sloane said between bites. 'For a start, the lady in charge of the catering was practically bowing in his presence and it was as if she could anticipate his every whim.'

'Honestly, I wish she'd leave me alone,' Lawrence said. 'I'm in danger of developing a bladder weakness with all that tea. It's not easy to get in and out of those blasted trousers with chaps attached, which Mrs Sparrow insisted I wear so I'd be used to them for tomorrow.'

Charlotte pretended to play the violin, causing the children to giggle. 'Oh, darling, it must be so hard having people fetch you tea all day,' she teased.

'And he had a masseuse on standby,' Lucas said.

'Come on.' Lawrence pouted. 'You know I've got a sore shoulder.'

'Anyone would have thought he was a movie

star or something,' Alice-Miranda said, wriggling her eyebrows.

In that moment, Imogen flicked a spoonful of chicken, hitting her father in the middle of his forehead.

'Movie star, my eye,' he laughed, and wiped the mush from his brow.

'How's the music coming along?' Venetia asked.

'Frau Furtwangler is a total slavedriver,' Caprice moaned. 'I thought Hairy and Trout were fussy, but Grizelda takes the biscuit. That boy Blade loves himself to bits too and don't even get me started on Sasha Goldberg. He is utterly hopeless.'

'I think he's just really nervous,' Millie said, leaping to the boy's defence. 'There must be a lot of pressure on him from his parents.'

'I'm sure he only got the part *because of* his parents,' Caprice scoffed. 'His singing is woeful. Blade is much better, although don't anyone tell him I said that. We don't need his head getting any bigger or we won't fit on the sound stage with him.'

'Might I say that this chicken is sensational,' Venetia said, eager to curtail her daughter's tirade. 'Could I be so bold as to ask you for the recipe?'

'Oh my Father God in heaven above me!'

Magdalena, who was hovering nearby, clutched at her chest and looked as though she were in pain, causing a few of the guests to jump to their feet. 'I have been terrified about what the great Missus Baldini would think of my cooking. And now you have paid me a compliment I will take with me to my grave.'

Everyone relaxed back into their chairs.

'Mummy is hopeless at cooking chicken,' Caprice announced. She speared a piece of potato with her fork and popped it into her mouth. 'It's always too dry. She drowns it in sauce to hide it, but really it's horrible.'

Venetia glowered at her daughter. 'It's good to know I've always got family in my corner.'

'Well, *you're* always telling me I should be truthful,' Caprice said, and placed her knife and fork together on her empty plate. She dabbed the corners of her mouth with her napkin and smiled sweetly.

'It would be my greatest pleasure to share my recipe with you, Missus Baldini,' Magdalena said in breathy gasps.

'Please, you must call me Venetia,' the woman said.

'All right, Missus Venetia, if you insist. I will write down the recipe for you now. But first I must telephone my sister and my cousin and tell them the great Missus Venetia likes my cooking.' And with that Magdalena rushed from the room.

As the family and friends returned to their dinner, talk circled back to the movie and the surprising change of director.

'I can't say I'm entirely happy about it,' Lawrence admitted. 'I've worked with Enzo Rossi several times before and he's a true artist. Andreas King seems pretty green.'

'That's because he's about fourteen,' Jacinta said.

'He appears to be a bit out of his depth,' Alice-Miranda added. 'There seems to be an awful lot of things to remember if you're the director and it can't help that Andreas has taken on such a huge task at the last minute.'

'Well, he must be good. Eli Goldberg is the executive producer and I'm sure he wouldn't hire just anyone,' Charlotte reasoned. 'That man has a formidable reputation.'

'True,' Lawrence conceded. 'He's far more cut-throat than his father, that's for sure.'

'Speaking of Abe and Dinah, I thought we

should ask them over for dinner before you head off to the canyon,' Charlotte said. 'I saw Dinah supervising Eduardo cutting the roses on the back fence yesterday and she mentioned that it would be great to meet the children. She was telling me about a trip she's planning with Abe. Apparently, it will be the first time they've been on a holiday since Eli was a boy. Poor woman, I get the feeling that the studio has always come first for Abe.'

'Are the Goldbergs your neighbours?' Caprice asked. Despite not being a fan of Sasha, she thought it couldn't do her career any harm to get to know his family better. What was that saying – it's not what you know but who you know?

Charlotte nodded. 'They live behind us on a magnificent old Hollywood estate, their home being the centrepiece. There's a residence for Sasha and his parents plus another beautiful house, although I'm pretty sure it's empty at the moment. Aviva is always dropping hints about the remodelling she'd like to do on the "big house".'

'You know Aviva, darling. If it sits still for long enough, she'll bedazzle it,' Lawrence said. 'Anyway, dinner with the Goldbergs is a fantastic idea. We can have a barbecue on the terrace.'

Charlotte glanced across the table and noticed Lucas looking as if he was fighting to keep his eyes open. Millie yawned widely, setting off a chain reaction around the dining table.

'Oh dear, I think you'll all be in bed as early as the twins,' the woman said. 'Your call sheet has you in wardrobe at half past six in the morning.'

Millie rubbed her eyes. 'I don't mind. I'm exhausted.'

Marcus and Imogen both yawned too.

'It looks like it's going to be a competition to see who can make it through dessert,' Lawrence commented. 'More for me, I say.'

At the mention of sweets, the children seemed to perk up.

Magdalena reappeared with a sheet of paper, which she handed to Venetia Baldini.

'Goodness me, you're a star, Magdalena. I didn't mean for you to write all that out now,' Venetia said. She scanned the page for the mystery ingredient.

The cook smiled. 'I would write my whole recipe collection for you if you want.'

Venetia frowned for a second. 'You know that's a very interesting idea.'

Magdalena beamed. 'As soon as I clear these

plates, would everyone like some macarons?' Venetia had picked some up that afternoon from the shop she'd discovered on her earlier outing with Aviva and Tish. 'I hope you don't mind, Missus Venetia, but I have made some of my especial vanilla bean ice-cream to go with them.'

Venetia smiled. 'That sounds delicious.'

'Ice cweam!' Marcus clapped his hands together, and everyone laughed.

'Me too!' Imogen shouted.

Chapter 15

The next morning, the children's first stop on set was the mind-boggling wardrobe department. Spread across three mezzanine floors, the costumes from hundreds of films were archived according to the year the film was made and the genre of the movie. The children were given a quick tour, marvelling at the racks upon racks of dresses, shirts, pants, hats, shoes and every other type of garment imaginable. A great portion of the middle floor was devoted to pattern makers and seamstresses and, according to the wardrobe mistress, a bird-like woman called Mrs Sparrow, the department was much smaller than it had once been.

When the children came upon the costumes from the famous movie *Ben Hur*, they couldn't resist trying on the helmets and marching around pretending to be Roman generals. Mrs Sparrow, meanwhile, had made it all the way to the next floor before she realised she'd lost her entire party and scurried back to find them. The children had prepared themselves for a scolding, but the woman had smiled and said she'd known exactly where they'd be. The Roman soldiers' costumes were everyone's favourites to try on.

The children were then led to a row of change rooms where their costumes were hanging on special timber hangers with their names neatly printed and attached. It didn't take long before everyone was kitted out and admiring their outfits. All except for Caprice, of course, who whined that her boots were pinching her toes. Mrs Sparrow hurried over to investigate and soon discovered that there was still some packing in them from a previous production where the actor must have had much smaller feet.

'I thought these would be brand-new, just for me,' Caprice said, horrified.

'Sorry, dear – a lot gets recycled on a movie set and I believe these boots were actually made decades ago for another film. They're a testament to buying quality products,' Mrs Sparrow said. 'And I don't suspect they've been worn terribly much, judging by their soles. Please take care of them. They're precious.'

Caprice wrinkled her nose. She still didn't like the idea that someone else's smelly feet had been in her boots.

Once the children were dressed, they were escorted to an adjacent building to have their hair and make-up done. A long room played host to at least two dozen work stations, each with a chair and mirror surrounded by naked light bulbs and a bench in front. There was a hair stylist and make-up artist allocated to each station. Sloane could hardly believe that the area was only for the extras and more minor actors. There were individual rooms for the big stars.

The hive of activity was overseen by Jerome Menzel, a tall man who had a habit of flicking his sleek black ponytail from side to side as he marched up and down the aisle, making sure that everyone's look was perfection. He also had the most impressive southern drawl and wore tight leather pants paired with a loud orange shirt.

Despite another spot of prima donna behaviour from Caprice, who wasn't at all happy with her hairstyle and demanded to have it redone twice, the children were on set only an hour and a half after they'd arrived.

'Good morning, Mr Lipp,' Alice-Miranda called, tipping her cowboy hat.

The man who was dazzling in a buttercup-yellow suit with a pink shirt and matching suede shoes. He was standing with Frau Furtwangler in the middle of a sea of music stands and chairs. 'Hello Alice-Miranda,' he said cheerfully. 'What an exciting day this is. And don't you all look fabulous.'

Alice-Miranda loved her cowgirl outfit. She wore her hair tied back in pigtails beneath a cowboy hat, a cream shirt with elaborate pink embroidery at the top, a fringed suede vest, jeans and boots. The girl couldn't help feeling as though she should jump on a horse and ride towards a sunset, which was exactly what they were going to be doing at the Grand Canyon in a few days' time. When Millie and Alice-Miranda had read the location scenes in their script, they'd both squealed with excitement. Sloane, on the other hand, had requested a stunt double for the riding scenes. Apparently, they could all have one, but there was no way that was going to happen for Alice-Miranda and Millie. Even Jacinta had decided to give it a go. After her experience with the Wongs' acrobatic show in China, the idea of being a stunt woman held a certain attraction for her.

'I bet Mr Lipp's glad he didn't live in the times of the Wild West,' Millie said quietly to Jacinta and Sloane.

'Why not?' Jacinta asked. She was enjoying the way her fringed vest swished and swayed as she moved.

'Way too much brown,' Millie said, pointing to their costumes.

Sloane giggled into her hand. 'That's true. Although at least we have coloured neckerchiefs.'

'Good morning, Frau Furtwangler,' Alice-Miranda called. The woman acknowledged her with an impatient wave.

'I don't think she likes working with children very much,' Sloane whispered to Millie.

Grizelda Furtwangler turned her head sharply and stared at the girl. 'Vot makes you say that?' she barked.

There it was again, the woman's bionic hearing – Sloane had barely breathed the words aloud. Harold

Lipp watched on, wondering what Grizelda was going to say.

Sloane shrugged. 'Um, just a feeling,' she said.

Millie braced herself for the onslaught.

'If it is because I am demanding and have high expectations, then you can interpret that as you vill, but I do not do average. If that is vot you aspire to be, I suggest you leave the production immediately.' The woman arched a heavily drawn eyebrow.

'I'm not going anywhere and I'm not average,' Sloane said stubbornly. She'd been working terribly hard to learn her lines and was determined to do a good job. Being accused of mediocrity didn't sit well with her at all. 'My accent is perfect now.'

Alice-Miranda took a deep breath and smiled at the musical director. 'Sloane was only saying last night what a fantastic challenge this experience is proving to be. Weren't you, Sloane?' she said. 'And I think we all realised yesterday, Frau Furtwangler, that you're very keen to get the best out of us.'

'Oh, and isn't she doing exactly that?' Mr Lipp gushed.

Grizelda glared at the man. 'You do not need to say anythink, Mr Lipp. But I am glad that you understand.' The woman tilted her head to the side and several ringlets flopped down onto her face. Alice-Miranda couldn't help noticing that Mr Lipp had barely taken his eyes off Frau Furtwangler even when she told him to be quiet, and yesterday his attention had been unwavering despite her barking at him at least ten times. She hoped the poor man wouldn't have to endure another dose of unrequited love, seeing that Mr Lipp had fancied Miss Reedy before she married Mr Plumpton.

The girls hurried to join the rest of the group.

Wade was looking at his watch and thinking about whether their wunderkind director was planning to join them anytime soon. 'Has anyone seen Mr King?' he asked the crew, who all shook their heads. 'Well, we can't start filming without him, but we could do a run-through.'

A minute later the children were stationed around the set. Wade called 'action' and Caprice, in character as Nellie, flounced out onto the porch of the biggest house in the row. She was clutching a wicker basket in her hands as she skipped down the steps and up the street towards the mercantile. Unlike the other girls, she wore a beautiful moss-green satin dress. Her long copper tresses had been curled and held in place with a matching bow. She completely ignored the children who were playing in the street until she spotted Sophie among the group and marched towards her. From Caprice's body language, her character wasn't at all happy with the situation. She wagged her finger at Sophie and told her to go home. She hadn't noticed Blade's character perched on the roof of a building opposite. He fired a pebble at her with a slingshot, thwacking her in the back of the head.

'Ow!' Caprice screeched. She dropped her basket and stamped her foot, then spun around and stared up at her attacker. 'You weren't supposed to actually hit me, you know!' she howled.

The boy peeked over the top of the fancy railing and grinned. 'Sorry, sometimes you get lucky,' he said without a hint of apology in his voice.

Millie, who was standing outside the mercantile, started to laugh.

'Well, don't do it again!' Caprice shouted, which only made more of the children giggle and some of the crew too.

'I think we've got a live one here,' a camera-man whispered to the boom operator standing next to him.

Wade walked onto the set and picked up the

offending missile. He turned it over in his hand and ran his finger along the jagged edges. 'It seems as though real pebbles have been mixed in with the fake ones,' he said, his mouth set in a grim line. 'Can we get someone from props to take a look at this, please?'

Andreas King finally wandered into the building. He certainly didn't appear to be a man in a hurry, despite being over an hour late. 'Morning, everyone. Love the threads, kids. You're all looking so wild and west.' Andreas smiled. 'But what's with the Oompa Loompa make-up?'

The children wondered what he meant. From where they were standing under the lights they all seemed completely fine.

'What are you talking about, Mr King?' Wade asked impatiently.

Andreas took a sip of his organic soy decaf latte. 'Come out here and take a look,' he replied.

Wade tried to hide the disdain he already felt for Andreas and joined him a few metres back from the set. As soon as he clapped eyes on the children, Wade gasped. 'You've got to be kidding me! Someone call hair and make-up, will you? Stat!'

Emmy had just arrived with a woman from

the props department and couldn't believe her eyes either. 'Oh wow,' she said, recoiling.

The children left their places around the town and gathered together in the middle of the street. They still couldn't see what the matter was.

Jerome stormed into the building. 'What is it? What in heaven's name is the problem? I was about to commence – eek!' He stumbled backwards at the sight of the children. 'What did you do to them?'

'Me? No, I think the better question is what did *you* do, Jerome?' Wade said evenly.

Alice-Miranda scurried off the set to see what all the fuss was about. She was shocked to find her friends' faces were glowing and not in a good way. 'We're green!' she exclaimed.

The children took turns running off the set to see for themselves.

'You're going to have to take them and start again, and this time don't get your monster make-up muddled in with your regular stuff,' Wade said. 'Can we meet back here in an hour?'

Jerome pressed the heel of his palm against his forehead. 'What do I look like? A magician?'

'You'd better hope so,' Emmy said, consulting her schedule for the day. 'We've got heaps to get through and the children are only here for the week. If we don't stay on track, this movie is not going to happen.'

Jerome threw his hands into the air. 'The things you ask of me, I cannot even . . . but I'll do it because I am a professional.' He strutted towards the door, his leather pants squeaking.

Andreas King hadn't said a word. He was flipping through the script and barely paying attention to the shenanigans unfolding in front of him.

'Andreas, would you like to brief the crew while the children are having their make-up redone?' Wade asked.

The young fellow shook his head. 'No, it's okay. I might get another hour's shut-eye. I'm just so tired,' he said, rubbing his eyes.

'Well, don't let us keep you,' Wade muttered.

'Thanks, man,' Andreas said, impervious to the fellow's sarcasm. 'If anyone needs me, I'll be in my bungalow – but only if it's an emergency. And could someone bring me a lobster thermidor and a glass of organic non-alcoholic red wine from Burgundy? That's in France,' he added.

As the children followed Jerome outside, there was much laughter and speculation about how they ended up looking like creatures from outer space.

'Andreas seems pretty relaxed about it all, don't you think?' Millie said to Alice-Miranda. 'If this was my chance to become a mega, hot-shot Hollywood director, I'd be spending every second getting to know how everything worked.'

Alice-Miranda frowned. 'I did wonder that, especially seeing that so many of us are also new to the game. I hope he hasn't taken on more than he can handle.'

Sasha was walking behind the girls. He hadn't caught the first part of their conversation and had only heard what Alice-Miranda had just said. The boy gulped. Everyone knew he was hopeless and they hadn't even started filming yet. He felt a gnawing guilt in the pit of his stomach. This movie meant so much to his grandfather and he was going to be the reason it was a disaster. He had to get himself fired as soon as possible so the project stood a fighting chance.

Chapter 16

The make-up debacle took almost two hours to fix. Whatever the team had used in the first place seemed to have set like concrete on the children's faces. Working out how to remove the goo was the first hurdle, and after several failed attempts, good old-fashioned cold cream proved to be the most effective option. It was Alice-Miranda who had suggested it. The child had remembered that, when she was very little, she'd had a fleeting predilection for drawing all over herself with permanent marker and Mrs Shillingsworth had found that cold cream worked like magic to clean it off. Unfortunately, studio stocks of the product were running low and it took another thirty minutes for one of the make-up artists to source some at a local pharmacy. Once the children's faces were clean, the process sped up again.

'Did you find out why we turned green, Mr Menzel?' Alice-Miranda asked, as the man strode around the chair she was sitting in, peering at her from all angles.

He shook his head and sighed as he knelt down to check the underside of her chin. 'You know, honey bunch, it's a total mystery. I ordered the same make-up I've been using on children for years, but this batch must have been mislabelled. I've spoken with my supplier and they're on their way over here to investigate. Between you and me, I'd hazard a guess that it's the curse of Nellie Williams.'

Alice-Miranda's interest was piqued immediately. 'What do you mean?' she asked.

'Oh, it's just old studio superstition,' Jerome said, batting his hand. 'Don't pay no mind.'

Back on the sound stage, Andreas King had woken from his nap and was wandering about, poking his head in and out of buildings, referring to the script and finally resembling director material.

'That was so weird about the make-up,' Sloane commented to Millie and Alice-Miranda as the girls walked along the street.

'I can't wait to see the pictures of us,' Millie said. 'Alien cowboys and cowgirls is kind of a fun idea. Maybe we should write a movie script about that – it could be our big break.'

'We'll have to show Chessie when we go back to school,' Sloane said. 'I wish she could have come with us too. I miss her a lot.'

Francesca Compton-Halls had joined the students at Winchesterfield-Downsfordvale this past term, having had quite an incredible adventure with Alice-Miranda and Millie in the last school holidays. Chessie, as she was known, had hit it off immediately with Sloane and during the term the pair had become inseparable. But given Chessie was only now getting to know her stepfather, Anthony Tavistock, she hadn't auditioned for the movie. Instead, she had opted to spend the holidays at her new home, Bagley Hall.

'I wonder if we'll get to perform a play with Fayle again this year,' Jacinta pondered aloud. She and Lucas were walking side by side behind the girls.

'Mr Lipp mentioned something in Drama about wanting to do *Romeo and Juliet*,' the boy said, then shyly added, 'We should try out.'

Caprice, who had been stealthily eavesdropping on the pair, wheedled her way around to Lucas's side. 'I know that part already,' the girl interjected. 'I think I'd be a shoo-in after starring in a Hollywood movie.'

'Of course you do,' Jacinta grumbled under her breath.

'I could definitely see you as Romeo,' Caprice said, linking her arm through Lucas's.

The boy flinched. He could feel Jacinta's eyes on him and didn't quite know what to do. He didn't want to be rude, but he also didn't want to encourage Caprice. He reached for Jacinta's hand on his other side, but she pulled away and stared ahead stonily. 'Uh, I just remembered I've got to tell Sep something about where we need to stand,' he said, wriggling out of Caprice's grasp and walking off in the opposite direction.

Caprice looked over at Jacinta and smiled.

'What's the matter? I thought you'd love it if Lucas became a star like his father.'

Jacinta refused to meet the girl's eye. 'Don't do that, Caprice,' she said through gritted teeth.

'What?' The copper-haired girl blinked innocently.

'You know exactly what I'm talking about,' Jacinta huffed, and stalked off to catch up to Alice-Miranda, Millie and Sloane.

'Whatever.' Caprice turned and waved at Lucas. It was fortunate that Jacinta didn't see the wink she gave him too.

Lucas quickly glanced away. He didn't know what the girl was playing at, but it gave him a very bad feeling. The last thing he wanted was another strange episode with Jacinta. He resolved to talk to her as soon as he could and do his best to stay well away from Caprice.

'Is she your girlfriend?' Blade asked, gesturing to Caprice.

Lucas looked at him in surprise and shook his head. 'No way.'

'That one's trouble with a capital "T",' Sep told him. 'Trust me, you don't want to go there.'

'But she's so . . .' Blade paused, searching for the right word.

Sophie rolled her eyes. 'Beautiful and talented?' she suggested. 'I think those are the words you were after.'

'She's something starting with a "b",' Lucas said.

'You mean a brat,' Sep jumped in.

'That's the one.' Lucas grinned. 'Why did you ask, Blade? Are you keen on her?'

Blade grimaced. 'She hates me.'

'Oh, the slingshot thing,' Sep said, nodding.

'I don't think that's the only reason and I wasn't trying to hurt her at all,' the boy said.

'She'll get over it,' Lucas assured him. 'And she's done way worse things to other people.'

Blade wondered if Caprice might seek revenge on him at some stage. He'd have to be on his toes, especially when they were on location. He'd heard that the Grand Canyon could be a dangerous place.

The line of children snaked its way along the road towards the sound stage as a trolley car full of tourists rounded the corner. They could hear the guide explaining over the loudspeaker that the children were filming a movie on the lot. Suddenly, there were at least twenty cameras trained on the group. The passengers waved and called hello. After the trolley car passed, the group was herded across the road and into the sound stage.

'Okay, everyone, we have an hour to get this scene right before Frau Furtwangler is due back with the orchestra. I need you all to pay attention and listen to Mr King's directions,' Emmy instructed.

This time Andreas King was a man on a mission. He had a clipboard and a headset and was racing about checking this and that with the cameramen and boom operators.

'He certainly looks ready for action now,' Alice-Miranda observed. 'Perhaps he was just exhausted from studying up on everything.'

'Okay, I need the cast on set in three minutes,' Andreas said. 'Let's do this thing.'

'Places, everyone,' Emmy called. She winked at the children. 'Break a leg.'

Caprice flounced off to take her position.

'You know you've got this,' Millie said to Sasha, and gave him a playful punch on the arm. The boy tried to muster a smile.

'Sasha Goldberg, hey man, where are you?' Andreas shouted across the set.

'Coming,' the boy said, and jogged to his position. He turned and gave Millie a wave. 'Thanks,' he mouthed.

'Oh, heck,' Andreas said, as Sasha reached him.

'Make-up!' he called. 'Can we get someone over here with a touch-up kit?' Beads of perspiration were trekking down the boy's temples. 'You gotta slow down, buddy, and take a breath. I can't have my leading fella all red cheeks and ears.'

'Sorry,' Sasha said. He could feel the damp under his arms too and had a horrible feeling that the dark shirt was soon going to look quite patchy.

'Your dad told me how you got this part blind – that the director before me didn't even know you were a Goldberg,' Andreas said.

'Really?' Sasha could feel a smile creeping onto his lips. In his mind, the only reason he'd got the part was because the director had been too scared not to give it to him. To hear that he'd earned the role on his own merit changed things. The boy puffed out his chest and nodded to himself. If that was the case, he'd better not let anyone down.

Blade was watching Sasha from his spot on top of the building. He'd overheard what Andreas had said. That was a lie if ever there was one.

Andreas checked that the children were all in position, then walked towards the crew. 'Action!' he yelled.

The children started the scene, but the crew

didn't move. The second assistant cameraman raced over and whispered in the director's ear. Andreas screwed up his face and smacked his hand against his clipboard. 'Stop! Stop, everyone!' he yelled. 'Go back to the start.'

Andreas seemed to be asking the man something else and then spent a minute talking to himself.

'Okay, I've got it now,' he muttered. He held up one finger and called 'roll cameras'. The sound recordist then shouted 'speed'. Andreas turned and looked at the set. The second assistant cameraman snapped the clapperboard and Andreas finally called, 'Action!'

Chapter 17

Tyger Lombardi placed the camera on the seat beside her. She wanted more than anything to get out of the car and stretch her legs, but having sat there for an hour and a half already, she didn't dare. It was Murphy's Law that the second she took a break she'd miss the shot, and a picture of Ethan Kane and his new girlfriend was worth more than she could afford to lose at the moment.

She rolled her head around her shoulders and stretched her arms, then picked up the camera and propped the lens on the open window. At least she had the place to herself today. Everyone else was off hunting shots of Lawrence Ridley and his co-star, Alexa Mills. She couldn't understand why. The stars were on a sound stage at Goldberg Studios and, short of infiltrating the crew, no one stood a chance of getting anywhere near them.

She had it on good authority – Ethan's pool cleaner, who she was paying far bigger tips to than he currently deserved – that his boss had gone out this morning in his new sports car and was due back before midday for his weekly appointment with his psychic. Ten years ago, the idea of a regular engagement with a clairvoyant who made house calls would have made Tyger laugh out loud, but she'd been in this town for too long now to even bat an eyelid. This was Hollywood – a weekly appointment with a snake charmer wouldn't have been unheard of.

Tyger hadn't had any more hostile visitors to the apartment since the weekend, but she was still wary. Thugs like that didn't give up easily and, while she'd dealt with plenty of creeps in her line of work, there was something about this fellow that worried her more than usual. She had been through every picture she'd taken in the past three months, trying to work out what he thought she had, but there was nothing out of the ordinary.

Tyger glanced at the clock in the centre of the dashboard. 'Come on, Ethan, I'm starving,' she said, as her stomach grumbled again. Besides getting something to eat, she wanted to swing by the *Stars Daily* headquarters to see whether they were going to use her shots of Charlotte Highton-Smith and the twins in this month's edition.

Tyger picked up her phone and was about to dial her contact to see if Ethan's plans had changed – the pool cleaner was good friends with the housekeeper, who had a hotline to Ethan's personal assistant – when a matte grey convertible roared into the street. She quickly lined up the camera and zoomed in as close as she could, training the crosshairs on the driver and his passenger.

Her patience was rewarded. From where she was sitting further up the road, and hidden by the car parked in front of her, it was obvious that Ethan and his new flame had no idea they were being photographed. She clicked away, taking hundreds of pictures. Then, quite unexpectedly, there was the money shot she couldn't have orchestrated better herself. As Ethan leaned over to give the woman a kiss, a gust of wind blew the man's luxurious crop of dark hair right off the top of his very bald head. The picture was gold as were the next few of him scrabbling to retrieve his toupee, not to mention the look of abject horror on his girlfriend's face.

Tyger shivered with excitement. With the money these pictures would bring on the open market, she might even be able to take a little holiday – no celebrities, no red carpets, just her and a beach and a good book. The car sped through the gates and disappeared. Tyger leaned over and carefully packed her camera away into the large bag on the seat beside her. She was about to start the car when a hand reached in through the open passenger window and seized the bag strap.

'Hey! What do you think you're doing?' Tyger yelled. She grabbed the camera bag with both hands and yanked as hard as she could, but she was no match for the hairy paw attached to the muscle-bound giant outside the car. The man pulled the bag through the window and out of her grasp. 'Give it back!' she demanded. 'I'm calling the cops.'

The fellow leaned on the windowsill. 'I don't think you will, and I'm happy to give it back as soon as you hand over what I want.'

Tyger looked at the man's face and froze. 'I – I don't know what it is that you think I have,' she stammered.

'The evidence, sweetheart,' he replied menacingly. 'So here's the deal. You give me the book and I'll give you your camera. I imagine you've got some pretty good shots of our famous friend on there. Shall we say Friday night?'

Tyger clenched her fists, trying to keep calm. 'What book?' she retorted.

'I'll be in touch. And if you choose not to play nice, Miss Lombardi, I can promise that things are going to get a lot worse for you.'

He stalked across the road towards a black SUV that looked like every other black SUV in town. Tyger reached for her phone. As the car sped away, she managed to get a couple of snaps, but realised afterwards that she'd aimed too high and missed the numberplate completely. The tinting was so dark there was no way of seeing inside.

Tyger smacked the steering wheel hard with both hands. 'Someone please tell me – give me a sign – what's the book?' she cried in frustration, garnering stares from a truck load of gardeners who had just pulled up to the mansion across the road. Maybe she should make an appointment with Ethan's clairvoyant.

Tyger needed her camera back – it was the most valuable thing she owned. She looked in the rear-vision mirror and fired up the engine. The one thing Tyger had was lots of books, but they were all hers as far as she knew. She'd been annoyed the other night that she couldn't find that J L Harvey book she'd bought on her birthday. The only possible explanation was that she'd lost it somewhere between the shops and the car. She'd have to turn her apartment inside out as soon as she got home. Maybe she could tidy up while she was at it. Heaven help her – things were getting way out of hand.

Chapter 18

'That's a wrap!' Andreas King declared.

The cameras stopped rolling and the children began to walk off set. Alice-Miranda had been watching the action intently while keeping in character. There was something bothering her about where Blade and Sasha had been standing. It didn't make sense at all. She hesitated, then decided there was no harm in asking.

'Excuse me, Mr King,' Alice-Miranda said, approaching the director.

Andreas looked up at her and smiled. 'Oh, hey. It's Alice-Matilda, isn't it? You're the friendly proper one.'

'Alice-Miranda,' she corrected pleasantly. 'I was wondering if I could have a look at the rushes.'

Intrigued, Andreas agreed and walked them over to a screen that was set up to the side of the cameras. 'Can you roll that?' he asked the video assist, who was wearing black jeans and a T-shirt that seemed to be playing host to the remains of his lunch.

Alice-Miranda watched as the scene unfolded in front of her. 'Could you stop it just there?' the child asked the operator, a minute into the footage.

Andreas peered at the screen. 'Is there a problem?'

'See where Blade is standing?' Alice-Miranda pointed to the screen. 'It seems he's blocking our view of Sasha. Given that Sasha's the star and his body language is really important here, perhaps it might be better to reposition them,' the girl said.

Neither Alice-Miranda nor Andreas realised there was an elderly gentleman now standing behind them. In his immaculate three-piece suit, which was adorned with a gold fob watch on a chain, he looked as if he could have walked straight off a 1940s movie set. He was listening intently to the exchange and was frankly stunned by the child's perceptiveness and the director's incompetence. 'May I take a look?' he asked.

Alice-Miranda and Andreas turned towards him.

'Oh, hey Mr Goldberg,' the operator said. 'Great to see you. It's been a while.' He replayed the segment and the old man nodded his head.

'I do believe you are right, young lady,' the elderly gentleman said, his forehead furrowing.

Andreas rubbed his chin. 'Wow, I totally missed that.'

The skin around Mr Goldberg's eyes crinkled into a smile. 'It was lucky for you that someone was paying attention.'

'It's lovely to meet you, Mr Goldberg,' Alice-Miranda said, offering her hand. 'I'm –'

'Alice-Miranda Highton-Smith-Kennington-Jones,' he finished, much to the tiny girl's surprise. 'I have heard a great deal about you from your aunt and uncle and had been looking forward to meeting you in person.'

Alice-Miranda smiled up at him. She thought he had the kindest watery blue eyes. 'And I've been looking forward to meeting you too.'

Abe Goldberg eyeballed the young director. 'You'd better shoot that scene again or it's not going to make any sense at all. Maybe I should have Alice-Miranda directing this movie, if you're not up to the task.'

'Oh, I'm sure that Mr King is very capable at his job and I didn't mean to cause any trouble,' Alice-Miranda said. She hadn't imagined when she asked to see the clip that Mr Goldberg would have been looking over their shoulders.

'You're not at all,' Abe Goldberg said, glaring at the dishevelled director. 'I've had my doubts about this fellow, so I'm glad that someone is keeping an eye on him.'

Andreas King laughed. 'You're a funny guy, Mr Goldberg. You wait and see. This is gonna be the best movie this studio has ever made. Excuse me for a minute while I run to the little boy's room.'

Alice-Miranda took the opportunity to tell Mr Goldberg about how wonderful she thought the script was. 'This movie is really quite ground-breaking. There aren't many westerns made these days, not compared to the time of, say, the great John Wayne and, given it's also a musical, well, that's unusual too,' she prattled. 'I heard your son say that it was your pet project. It must be so rewarding to see a passion of yours come to life before your very eyes.'

Abe Goldberg swallowed hard. 'I suppose there are stories that you just have to get to the screen and this is one of them.'

On the set, Alexa Mills and Lawrence Ridley were having a run-through of the scene Andreas had been planning to shoot before they broke for lunch. As Alexa walked out of the mercantile, Abe Goldberg glanced up and gasped.

'Maura,' he whispered, a faraway look in his eyes.

Alice-Miranda followed his line of sight and saw that he was staring at Alexa Mills and mumbling something to himself. She wondered who Maura was.

Sasha rushed over from the other side of the building where he and the rest of the children had been enjoying a snack. 'Grandpa! Did you see me?'

Abe Goldberg snapped back to the present. He looked at the lad, whose smile couldn't have been any broader. 'What did you say, Sasha?'

'Did you see my scene?' the boy repeated.

His grandfather shook his head. 'You're going to have to shoot it again,' he said. 'This has to be right.'

Sasha's face fell. Up until now he thought he'd done well with it. 'Was there something the matter?' he asked, his bottom lip trembling.

Emmy rushed up to them, headset buzzing and clipboard in hand. 'Excuse me, Mr Goldberg, I've just been told you're needed back at the office immediately. Mrs Fairbrother said that Mr Winx and Mr Dalgety are here to see you.'

'Let them know I'm on my way.' The old man turned to Alice-Miranda. 'Make sure you keep an eye on our young director for me,' he said with a wink.

'I promise I will, and it was lovely to meet you, Mr Goldberg,' Alice-Miranda replied, and gave a wave. She saw Sasha wave at him too, but the man seemed to look straight through the boy. Alice-Miranda couldn't help but notice Sasha's sagging shoulders and the downcast expression on his face. The poor boy looked as though he needed some friends more than ever.

Chapter 19

'Isn't Emmy fabulous? I think she must be one of the bravest people I've ever met, apart from you, Alice-Miranda,' Millie said, as the vehicle headed out of the studio gates. The children were being driven home by Lawrence's driver, Bob, via a quick sight-seeing detour. Lawrence had stayed behind to shoot another scene with Alexa, but given things were running so far overtime, Emmy had put her foot down about moving the children's recording session to the following day.

Despite receiving a tirade of abuse, Emmy had stood her ground and reiterated that there were strict labour laws around children on film sets and she was not going to risk the wrath of the actors' union if they ran a minute over what they were allowed. Besides, she had reasoned, the children were exhausted and Frau Furtwangler couldn't possibly expect to get the best out of them in such a state.

'I love that she stood up to Grizzie,' Caprice said. 'That woman is a tyrant.'

'It was Mr Lipp I felt most sorry for,' Alice-Miranda said. 'Although he didn't seem too upset when Frau Furtwangler demanded he stay back and go through the score with her another three times.'

'He looked quite pleased, really. I think he might have a little bit of a crush on grumpy old Grizzie,' Millie said. She opened the small bar fridge that was built into the floor of the SUV and distributed bottles of water to her friends.

'No way!' Caprice blurted. 'She'd smoosh him with those big feet of hers. Plus, she hates everyone. And why would you like someone who doesn't like you at all? That's just stupid.'

'It's happened before. He used to carry a torch

for Miss Reedy,' Sloane said, twisting the cap off her drink.

Caprice wrinkled her lip. 'You're joking, right?'

'No, she's not. When we were in Paris for our choir trip, Mr Lipp said that he was going to ask Miss Reedy out and that's why Mr Plumpton finally got his act together,' Sep chimed in.

Jacinta grinned. 'Could you imagine Reedy and Hairy together? That would have been terrible. Everyone knew that Plumpy and Reedy were meant for one another, even when they couldn't see it for themselves.'

'So, you set them up?' Caprice was almost impressed.

The children nodded.

'And it worked out beautifully,' Alice-Miranda said. 'But I've always felt sad that Mr Lipp hasn't found his special someone. I've grown quite fond of him over the years. I think he has a very kind heart and he deserves to fall in love.'

'He needs a stylist,' Caprice quipped. 'Then perhaps he wouldn't blind potential dates with his technicolour outfits.'

Millie clasped her hands and tapped her fore-fingers together slowly.

'What are you thinking?' Alice-Miranda asked. She knew all too well when her best friend was formulating a grand plan.

Millie smiled mischievously. 'Just call me cupid.'

'Grizzie and Lipp sounds like a very bad idea,' Jacinta said.

Caprice chuckled. 'Grizzie and Hairy is a fantastic idea!'

The vehicle crawled onto the freeway ramp that led from Studio City back to Hollywood, easing into the procession that took up sixteen lanes, eight in either direction.

Jacinta looked at the lines of cars snaking their way up and down the hillside. 'I'm never going to complain about traffic ever again,' she sighed, leaning against the window.

'Didn't you say that when we were in China?' Lucas said. 'It was terrible there too, remember.'

'True, but this is a different type of terrible. The freeways here are even wider and it's still a car park,' Jacinta observed.

'It's okay, kids,' Bob piped up. 'I know a short cut a little further down. We won't have to spend long in this. I can point out some landmarks on the way if you'd like to learn more about the city.'

'That sounds great,' Alice-Miranda said.

'Boring,' Caprice muttered.

Jacinta turned and glared at the girl, who had been relegated to the very back seat of the Escalade. 'Well, you don't have to listen, you know.' Caprice had tried to get Lucas to sit with her, but the boy had escaped to the front, which had annoyed Jacinta no end. Although she was relieved he hadn't taken up Caprice's invitation, she would have much preferred he sit with her in the middle row.

'I know you saw the Hollywood sign on the way up this morning, but if you look to your left now, you can get another pretty good view of it,' Bob said.

'Is it true that it was once a real-estate sign?' Sep asked.

'I know the answer to that,' Millie jumped in. 'I read about it in my guide book. The sign originally said "Hollywood Land" and it was lit up with four thousand light bulbs. The sign was only supposed to stay for eighteen months because they were trying to sell the land above it, and at times it almost fell down. A while ago some local businessmen decided it should be rebuilt properly and now it's here for good.'

Bob grinned at her in the rear-vision mirror. 'You're absolutely right, Miss Millie – unless an earthquake says otherwise.'

'Oh yes, I almost forgot the whole of California sits over the San Andreas Fault,' Alice-Miranda said.

'I really don't want to think about that,' Sloane said, looking slightly peaky at the idea.

'Just down further in front of the sign is the Hollywood Reservoir, which forms part of the city's water supply,' Bob continued, swiftly changing the subject. 'You can go hiking around the area. There are some nice trails and the view is breathtaking.'

'Wow, the city water supply – who knew this tour would be so interesting?' Caprice grumbled.

Jacinta turned and glared at her again but chose not to say anything.

The traffic was starting to improve and it wasn't long before Bob left the freeway and the children found themselves on Hollywood Boulevard.

'I recognise where we are,' Alice-Miranda said, pressing her nose against the window. 'That's the Dolby Theatre and right next door is the famous Grauman's Chinese Theatre, where Uncle Lawrence said we'll probably have the premiere of our movie next year.'

'It's really cool,' Lucas said. 'I went there with Dad last time I was in town. And out the front along the street there are over two hundred handprints of Hollywood stars, as well as all the stars that make up the Walk of Fame.'

'I wonder if I'll get one of those,' Caprice mused.

Millie laughed out loud. 'I think you have to be a star to get a star. Lawrence has one, doesn't he?'

Lucas nodded. 'Yes, but it's further along. The stars are in Vine Street too.'

Caprice poked her tongue out at Millie, who fortunately didn't see it.

'Excuse me, Mr Loy, do you think we could hop out and take some photographs?' Alice-Miranda asked. 'Have you got your camera, Millie?'

'It's right here.' The girl rummaged around in her day pack and pulled it out. She'd asked Emmy if she could snap some pictures on set earlier but had then forgotten about it because they were so busy. It probably didn't matter as there seemed to be someone from the studio following the group, armed with a camera.

Bob found a spot right by Grauman's theatre, but he could only park there for a few minutes. The children piled out of the car and ran off in all directions to see as many of the stars as they could.

'You have to remember, kids, that lots of these people were famous in the Golden Age of Hollywood, long before you were born – heck, even before I was born for some of them,' Bob said, 'which means that many of them have passed on.'

Alice-Miranda wandered along, taking in the names. She stopped at one star. Maura Devine. It was the same name she'd heard Mr Goldberg call Alexa when she was on set today.

'Excuse me, Mr Loy,' Alice-Miranda said. 'Can you tell me about this lady here?'

Bob walked over to stand beside the child. 'Oh, she was a flame-haired beauty. One of the most talented stars in Hollywood in the late forties.'

'What happened to her?' Alice-Miranda asked.

Bob paused and scratched his head. 'You know, I can't remember exactly. I think there was some tragedy. I'd have to look it up for you.'

'Okay, gather around, everyone. I want some star power,' Caprice directed.

'Hey, it's my camera, so I get to call the shots!' Millie huffed. It was getting late in the day and tempers were clearly beginning to fray.

'Could you please take our picture, Mr Loy?'

Alice-Miranda took the camera from Millie and passed it to the driver.

Bob waited for the children to arrange themselves and then snapped away. Caprice struck several poses. She had her hands on her hips, then one hand in the air, then both hands resting under her chin.

'One last photograph, Bob,' Caprice said. She put her arm around Lucas and turned her face towards his cheek, puckering her lips.

'What do you think you're doing?' Jacinta shrieked, and pushed the girl away. 'Don't you dare!'

'What?' Caprice said. 'It was just a joke. When did you get a sense of humour bypass? Oh, that's right – you never had a sense of humour to begin with!'

Lucas's cheeks were alight as he stood between the two girls. Sep and Sloane were chuckling, which only seemed to make Jacinta angrier. Millie quickly took back her camera and scrolled through the shots. The right thing to do, she thought, was to delete the photo, but it was definitely the best shot of Grauman's Chinese Theatre in the background.

Sloane hurried over to take a look. 'It's actually a really good picture,' she said.

Jacinta was having none of it. 'Get rid of it,' she ordered.

'But I like it,' Millie said. 'And it's my camera.'

'Alice-Miranda, tell Millie to delete that picture,' Jacinta whined.

But Alice-Miranda was already scampering off to the entrance of the theatre, where she had spotted someone who looked vaguely familiar. It was a woman holding a camera and aiming it towards them. It was only the small, regular type a tourist would have, but suddenly the penny dropped and Alice-Miranda realised that this woman was no holiday maker.

'Excuse me,' the child called out, running towards Tyger Lombardi. 'Please stop taking photos of us. Aunt Charlotte will be furious and you'll most likely get into trouble. It's a dreadful invasion of privacy.'

Behind her, in the distance, Jacinta and Caprice were still squabbling and Bob was now trying to convince a parking inspector of all the reasons he should put his ticket pad away and let them go.

'Do you have any idea what it's like trying to make a living in this town?' Tyger sighed. 'Of course you don't. You're a kid without a care in the world and your parents are rich. As long as you have everything, why would you even consider anyone else's situation?'

'I don't think that's a particularly fair assessment, Miss Lombardi. You don't know anything about me,' Alice-Miranda pointed out.

'Well, what makes you such an expert on me then?' Tyger retorted. She wished she'd bothered to wear a clean pair of jeans and wash her hair that morning. Just being in the presence of this kid made her feel even scruffier than usual.

'I know that you tried to sell private photographs of the twins, and Aunt Charlotte was very upset about it,' the child said.

'I was about to be booted out of my apartment that week. I needed the money, and if you think I'm proud of that, I can tell you I'm not,' Tyger said. 'It certainly wasn't my finest hour.'

'I don't understand then. If you're not proud of what you do, why do you do it?' Alice-Miranda asked.

Tyger shrugged. 'Look, sweetheart, sometimes you think life is going to take you in one direction and then – whammo! – your hopes and dreams are crushed. But you still have to eat and pay the rent.'

'Perhaps if you asked nicely instead of

ambushing people, they might give you what you're after and everyone would be happy,' Alice-Miranda suggested.

'Oh, princess, don't you just live in a fairytale,' Tyger said nastily.

Bob had managed to talk his way out of a ticket and was now corralling the kids into the car before the officer had a change of mind. Caprice elbowed Jacinta out of the way and clambered to the very back seat. Sep and Sloane climbed in after her while Millie hopped into the front, leaving Lucas no choice but to sit next to Jacinta.

'Alice-Miranda, we have to go,' Millie called.

Alice-Miranda gave a wave to indicate that she was on her way. She turned back to Tyger Lombardi to say goodbye, but was stopped by the expression on the woman's face. She looked as if she'd seen a ghost. Before Alice-Miranda had a chance to ask if she was all right, Miss Lombardi ran away, disappearing into a large group of tourists.

Alice-Miranda scanned the crowds in search of what had spooked the woman. Her gaze settled upon a tall, muscly man who also seemed to be searching for someone. With her suspicions on high alert, Alice-Miranda walked over to him. 'Excuse me, sir, I was wondering if you could tell me about this chap here,' she said, pointing at a star on the footpath.

He peered down at the child. 'What? Are you talking to me?'

'Yes, I am. You see, I'm interested to know about this fellow, Mr Abe Goldberg,' she said. 'And you look like you might know about these things.'

'Biggest fool in Hollywood,' the man said without so much as a bat of an eyelid. 'Get out of my way, kid. I'm meeting someone.' He craned his neck, scanning the spot Tyger was last seen, and lumbered through the throng of visitors.

'Alice-Miranda, come on,' Millie called again. 'There's going to be blood spilled in this car soon if you don't hurry up.'

Alice-Miranda watched as the man searched and searched. The look on his face said it all. He was flushed from the neck up and his hands were balled into fists. Tyger Lombardi was clearly terrified of him. Alice-Miranda knew that it was none of her business, but she had a strange feeling and she was usually right about her strange feelings. She scurried to the edge of the footpath and jumped into the back of the Escalade. Caprice was sobbing, Jacinta was crying and Lucas was sitting there looking like he'd been slapped with a wet fish.

Alice-Miranda grimaced. 'Oh dear, what did I miss?'

Chapter 20

The next morning flew past. By eleven-thirty, the children's section of the score had been recorded and Frau Furtwangler even deigned to tell them they'd done quite a good job, although she wanted Sasha, Blade and Caprice to stay behind to do some more work on their solos.

'But my part was perfect,' Caprice grouched. 'Mr Lipp told me so.'

Frau Furtwangler clasped her hands together and walked over to the girl. She leaned down to speak with her quietly. 'Vell then, perhaps I should find someone else to sing your part.' The woman took a step back and surveyed the group. 'You vith the long hair – vot is your name?'

Sophie looked up from the book she was reading, surprise and a hint of fear etched into her features. 'Me?'

'Yes, you, the reader,' Grizelda barked.

As the quietest member of the cast, Sophie spent her spare time on set reading. She had been engrossed in a book about dogs because her parents had promised her a pug for her next birthday. The girl began to shake like a blancmange at being addressed directly by Frau Furtwangler. Everyone knew the frau didn't indulge in conversation. The musical director's preferred mode of communication was shouting, and if she singled you out, it was almost always because you were in trouble.

The woman narrowed her eyes. 'You can sing. I have heard your voice and you are good. Perhaps not as good as this canary here, but it vill do. Do you vant her solos?'

Caprice baulked. 'But her voice is nothing like mine!' she protested. 'I'm *spectacular*. I won the National Eisteddfod.'

'Runner-up this year, I believe,' Millie quipped, earning herself a look from the girl that would have frozen fire.

'Vell then,' Frau Furtwangler said. 'I am sure you von't mind staying behind and doing some more vork to make sure that you are as perfect as you think you are.'

Caprice knew she was defeated. 'I'll need one of my friends to keep me company. I want . . .' There was a pregnant pause and Jacinta made a grab for Lucas's arm. Caprice looked around and seemed to be thinking for quite a long time about what she was going to say. 'I want Alice-Miranda because she always makes me feel better and we're best friends.'

'Since when?' Millie whispered, hurt.

Alice-Miranda squeezed Millie's hand and gave her a reassuring smile.

'At least she didn't ask Lucas to stay,' Millie conceded. 'It would have been World War Three if that had happened.'

Last night, after they had arrived home, Caprice had stalked off to the guesthouse and flatly refused to join them for dinner, even though her mother and Magdalena had whipped up a veritable feast. Jacinta was still cross and poor Lucas was left feeling like the meat in the sandwich. It had taken a barrage of Lawrence's lame dad jokes to coax a smile out of the girl as well as Lucas promising that Caprice never even touched his face. When Millie showed the picture to the rest of the family, the fact that they'd found it amusing hadn't helped.

Emmy was listening to her headset and scribbling on the notepad that seemed permanently attached to the crook of her left arm. 'Okay, kids, the bus is here to take you to the park,' she said. 'You'll be accompanied by Eric and Gemma, who are two of our amazing guides up there.'

'If you're staying then I'll stay too,' Millie said to Alice-Miranda. 'They're only going for a couple of hours anyway. I'm sure we can guilt Lawrence into taking us for a whole day before we go back home.'

'It's a deal,' Alice-Miranda replied, giving her best friend a hug.

While the rest of the children exited the sound stage, Caprice stood there with her jaw flapping. 'So, you're really going to stay here with me?' she asked.

Alice-Miranda nodded. 'I thought that's what you wanted?'

'And I'm staying too,' Millie said, folding her arms across her chest. 'So *Alice-Miranda* has some company.'

'I didn't think you'd do it. Now I feel a bit bad,' Caprice said. 'But not that bad. Hardly at all, actually.'

Alice-Miranda stifled a smile. The mere fact that Caprice felt bad for anyone had to be a good sign. Maybe the girl was learning to think about others, although probably not quite at the right time.

Frau Furtwangler thumbed through the score-sheets. 'Enough of this namby-pamby nonsense. I vant to take your solos from the top – first you and you,' she said, pointing at Caprice and Sasha. She then turned to Mr Lipp. 'I require a glass of varm vater between the range of thirty-two and thirty-seven degrees vith a twist of lemon and a pinch of lime and half a teaspoon of honey, vich must be added at room temperature and drizzled from an exact height of ten centimetres above the glass.'

Harold Lipp danced about on the spot, wondering where he would source those ingredients.

'Do not continue to stand there – go and get it for me!' Grizelda demanded. 'And bring me some headache tablets too. My temples are pounding.'

'We'll help you if you like, sir,' Alice-Miranda offered.

'Good idea,' Millie said, seizing the chance to get out of there.

The two friends walked over to Emmy, who explained that the bungalows were located in the cul-de-sac across the road and off to the left and it wouldn't take more than a couple of minutes to get there.

'Is anyone getting my drink?' Grizelda roared, 'or vill I die standing here, vaiting for it?'

'We're on our way!' Mr Lipp called, as he and the girls hurried out of the building.

Chapter 21

Mr Lipp and the girls turned right then left into the little dead-end street that rolled away down the hill. All of the bungalows were marked with large numbers, although oddly enough number one wasn't actually the first in the street.

'So, *this* is where Frau Furtwangler is staying while we're shooting the movie.' Millie let out a low whistle as they stepped into the bungalow.

'It's jolly nice,' Mr Lipp said, taking in the plush furnishings. The lounge area was decorated in the most tasteful creams and beiges. 'But, if it were up to me, I'd add a few splashes of colour.'

'Is your flat at school as colourful as your wardrobe, sir?' Millie asked. While the children often raised their eyebrows at his choice of clothing, Millie couldn't help but admire the man's commitment to his own sense of style.

'It's a technicolour dream, Millicent – utterly spectacular!' The man grinned, and Millie did too.

By the time they had made their way to the kitchen, Alice-Miranda had located lemons and limes in a basket on the bench and a jar of honey in the cupboard. She flicked on the kettle and immediately set about making Frau Furtwangler's requested beverage while Mr Lipp found a tray to carry it all on. When Alice-Miranda was finished, she checked to make sure the kitchen was just as tidy as when they'd arrived. She washed and dried the knife she'd used and put it away in the drawer.

'Now, we need to find headache tables,' the tiny child said, tapping her chin.

'Why don't I take this and you girls can find them and follow me?' Mr Lipp said, aware that the warm water was cooling every second they delayed.

'I don't want the temperature to be incorrect – Frau Furtwangler was very specific.'

'Good idea,' Alice-Miranda said, and decided to try the bathroom. She pushed open a pair of double doors into a beautiful bedroom. It was appointed with lavish furnishings and in the middle of the bed were the fluffiest cushions she had ever seen.

Millie couldn't resist and grabbed one, nuzzling, it against her face. 'What do you think these are made from?' she said. 'I've never felt anything so soft.'

'Probably the flaxen hair of seventeen maidens woven with chinchilla and cashmere and the breath of twenty-five newborn babies,' Alice-Miranda said, running her hand over the fabric.

Millie laughed. 'Wow, and here I was thinking it was some goat or a lamb or something far more ordinary.'

Alice-Miranda giggled and skipped to the enormous en-suite bathroom, which was a vision of grey and white marble. There was a huge bathtub and a shower with dual showerheads. The vanity unit took up a whole wall and hidden in another small room was a toilet.

Millie threw the cushion back onto the bed and followed her friend. She opened one of the shaving cabinet's mirrored doors and triumphantly declared that she had found the medication. Her eyes swept across the range of medications that filled the shelves. Together, Alice-Miranda and Millie checked the boxes and located some paracetamol and ibuprofen, which were both for headaches. The girls decided it was better to go armed with choices rather than have to come back again.

Alice-Miranda closed the cabinet door while Millie spotted an elegant bottle of perfume she couldn't resist squirting onto her wrists when the sound of footsteps echoed from the sitting room.

'Hairy must have come back – oops!' Millie grabbed a towel and tried to rub off the scent. Alice-Miranda was about to call out to Mr Lipp when the girls heard two voices they didn't recognise. One was gruff and gravelly and didn't sound particularly friendly.

'So, what are you going to do if she doesn't come up with the goods on Friday night?' a man said.

'I suppose I'll just make her go away – permanently – although we'll still need to find it,' the other fellow replied.

The girls looked at one another and frowned. 'Who are they going to make disappear?' Millie whispered. She didn't like the sound of this at all.

'Are you sure she's got it?' the first voice said.

'Tyger Lombardi is one wily customer.'

Millie and Alice-Miranda's eyes widened at the mention of the infamous paparazzo.

'She's got it all right, and we need to get it back before she realises exactly what she has. Although she could already know its value and have been playing us this entire time. If that's the case, I expect it's going to cost the boss a lot of money to buy her silence – or we could do things my way and we can pick up the loot instead.'

As the men neared, Alice-Miranda pointed at the door that led into the separate toilet. Millie nodded, and the two girls tiptoed across the marble floor, trying not to make a sound.

'Where are you going to hide that thing?' the first man asked.

'In here, I guess.'

The footsteps came closer. Alice-Miranda pressed herself against the wall while Millie hid on the other side of the toilet. The girls had heard too much and these men probably wouldn't take kindly to eaves-droppers, no matter how innocent their intentions.

'Hey, I thought you said this bungalow was empty,' said one of the men. 'There's a wardrobe full of women's clothing and a toiletries bag in here too.'

Alice-Miranda and Millie both held their breath as footsteps fell in the bathroom.

'This is bungalow three, isn't it?' the other man said. There were more footsteps before he called from the door. 'This is bungalow one, you bozo. Let's get out of here before someone sees us.'

His accomplice took another step into the bathroom. Alice-Miranda was expecting to be discovered any second.

'Hey, what are you doing?' the fellow at the door hissed.

'Keep your hair on. I just wanted to check out the tiles. They're beautiful.' The man pulled the bathroom door but didn't close it completely. 'And it smells lovely in there. What? A guy can't appreciate nice things?'

Millie bit down on her lip, trying not to giggle. When they were sure that the men had gone, she let out a deep breath. 'I thought he was going to say he needed to pee,' she confessed. 'That would have been the end of us.'

'Let's see if we can get a look at them,' Alice-Miranda said, hurrying to the sitting room. She motioned for Millie to stay low to the ground, and the pair crossed the floor on their hands and knees, popping up in the corner of the window by the drapes. Alice-Miranda gasped.

'What's the matter?' Millie said, sneaking a glimpse at the two men. One had muscles on his muscles with a dark complexion and bald head. The other was shorter and a lot softer around the edges with a mop of caramel curls.

'I saw that bald man out the front of Grauman's Chinese Theatre yesterday, when I caught Tyger Lombardi taking our pictures,' Alice-Miranda said.

'You didn't tell me that,' Millie rebuked.

'I would have except that you had your hands full playing referee between Jacinta and Caprice,' Alice-Miranda replied. 'Tyger looked scared and now I know why. It sounds like those men are after her for something terribly serious.'

'But what can we do about it?' Millie asked. 'We don't know who those guys are or who they work for. They mentioned "the boss", but that could be anyone.'

'Maybe it's best we tell Uncle Lawrence and he can see if she needs help,' Alice-Miranda said.

'I don't think she's your aunt and uncle's favour-ite person. She's probably done something awful, but in the meantime, we could do some investigating of our own.' Millie waggled her eyebrows.

Alice-Miranda's frown disappeared as she broke into a grin. 'You've been watching too many detective movies.'

'Well, if you can't be a detective on a movie set, where can you?' Millie said.

'Come on then, we'd better get back.' Alice-Miranda took Millie's hand and Frau Furtwangler's headache tablets.

'Good idea,' Millie said, wincing at the thought of incurring the woman's wrath. 'Grizelda's scary enough without a sore head.'

And with that, the pair raced out the door.

Chapter 22

Millie kept an eye out as they charged up the hill towards the sound stage, but the men were nowhere to be seen. The girls entered the building, garnering a glare from Frau Furtwangler. She looked to have downed half the pitcher of water, which was sitting on a small table beside the grand piano. Mr Lipp hurried over and took the tablets from the girls. 'You'd better take a seat,' he said quietly.

Alice-Miranda and Millie sat down as far from the woman as they could.

Millie motioned to the door with her eyes. 'Do you think we could go outside?'

'Quiet!' Frau Furtwangler ordered. She slugged back two headache tablets and rubbed her temples. 'Nobody speak – I am a voman on the edge. On second thoughts, nobody breathe.' She closed her eyes and rolled her head on her shoulders. For a minute or so, you could have heard a pin drop. Suddenly, Grizelda's eyes sprang open and it was business as usual. 'Now, Caprice, I vant you to sing that section again and this time Blade vill do the harmony.'

Millie looked over at Sasha, who didn't seem terribly upset about being usurped from his role. 'Poor kid,' she whispered. 'Why did he even get the part if Grizzie isn't going to use him?'

An external door opened just as Caprice and Blade reached the crescendo. Alice-Miranda felt tingles run up and down her spine while she listened to the beautiful sounds. Mr Lipp was standing with his eyes closed, drowning in the perfect notes.

'That sounds like them,' a woman declared loudly.

Millie and Alice-Miranda turned to see Aviva Goldberg trip-tripping across the concrete floor in a towering pair of sparkling lime heels. 'Oh my gawd,

I don't think I've ever heard Sasha sound so good. That Grizelda Furtwangler sure knows how to get the best out of –' Aviva stopped in her tracks as she stared at Blade in confusion. 'What's going on? Why is Blade singing instead of Sasha?'

Frau Furtwangler rose to her feet. 'Mrs Goldberg, you are not allowed on set, so please leave before I call security to have you removed.'

'I will not be going anywhere. Not until I find out exactly what is happening here. How dare you replace my son with this boy! It's not his part!' Aviva quivered like a jelly on a plate.

The older woman standing beside her didn't look happy either. Tish Crawford, on the other hand, could barely disguise her excitement.

'Emmy, get my husband in here right away!' Aviva barked.

Emmy spoke quickly into her headset. Mr Goldberg would be furious about his wife infiltrating the set, but his reaction to Frau Furtwangler replacing Sasha was a whole other level of concern.

Frau Furtwangler looked at the clock on the wall and sighed. 'Ve do not have time for this nonsense. You must leave immediately. I vill not have my recording ruined.'

The door banged open and Eli Goldberg's heavy footsteps echoed around the sound stage. 'Aviva, I told you that there were no parents on set, so what are you doing back here?' he yelled, then sobered as he realised that she had not come alone. 'Oh, hello Mother. What are you doing here?' He greeted her with a kiss.

Dinah Goldberg was a lesson in understated elegance, dressed in a navy pant suit. She was about to speak when Aviva waved a bejewelled hand and said, 'Your mother and I were showing Tish around and thought we'd drop by to see how the kids were doing and it was just as well we did. *This* woman has robbed our son of the lead part!'

Eli marched up to Frau Furtwangler. 'Why is that boy singing Sasha's part?' he demanded. If he was trying to intimidate the woman, it wasn't going to work. She towered over the top of him by at least three inches.

She leaned down until her nose was almost touching his. 'Mr Goldberg, vould you remind me who is the musical director of this film?'

'You are,' he replied grudgingly, but Eli could be as stubborn as the next person and was determined not to cave in.

'So, I am making my decisions and unfortunately your son has a voice like a squealing pig,' she stated matter-of-factly. 'As you know, I am a genius, but sadly my talent does not extend to that of a miracle vorker.'

'How dare you!' Aviva's jaw flapped open and you could almost see the steam pouring from her ears. 'Sasha is spectacular. His grandmother says so all the time. Don't you, Dinah?'

The woman nodded. 'Yes, my grandson is a rare talent.'

Sasha could feel tears pricking his eyes. He was doing his best to stem the tide, but it was a losing battle. He brushed at his face. Millie and Alice-Miranda looked at each other before Millie jumped up and ran over to comfort the boy. Emmy gulped and Mr Lipp wrung his hands together in anticipation of what was to come.

'My son will sing his part,' Eli said. He spoke calmly and without any trace of anger, although his ears and the back of his neck had now graduated from pink to red. It was not a suggestion but a command and both of them knew it.

'Yes, our son has the lead and you will do what my husband says. He's the boss of this studio,' Aviva said, quaking with anger.

Emmy could see Dinah Goldberg press her lips together tightly and wondered if Aviva's declaration that her husband was in charge had upset her. Tish Crawford's smugness was disappearing faster than the pay packet she had been counting on for her son. But Tish wasn't the only one feeling like a loser. Grizelda Furtwangler could see the Academy Award she'd been dreaming of slipping from her grasp. There was only so much she could do to mask the flat tone and bum notes that Sasha had laid down. Caprice wished they'd hurry up and get on with it. She was busting to go to the loo.

'But, Dad, I . . . I'm okay with Blade singing that part,' Sasha mumbled. 'If we record his voice and I lip-sync it in the film, no one will even know.'

Eli Goldberg rested his hands on his son's shoulders and looked him straight in the eye. Millie shuffled a little to the left so as not to get in the way. 'I would know and your mother and your grandparents too. Is that what you want? It would be a lie, Sasha,' Eli said.

'But this is the movies, Dad. It's all a lie, isn't it? And it's not like it hasn't happened before.' Sasha couldn't believe he'd said that. It was the first time in his life that he'd ever stood up to his father, and although he shuddered to think what was going to happen next, it felt good.

Eli sighed. 'You've got a lot to learn, Sasha, and if you're going to become the big star that you've always wanted to be, you need to suck it up and carry on. So what if your voice isn't quite as good as that kid's? You earned this part and now you're going to see it through. You're a Goldberg, you're not a quitter.'

'No, us Goldbergs don't quit,' Aviva said.

Dinah Goldberg caught her grandson's eye and slowly shook her head, leaving the boy in no doubt as to her feelings on the matter.

Eli turned on his heel and left the building with Aviva, his mother and Tish in tow.

Sasha tried to remember when exactly he'd mentioned that he wanted to be a big star. He looked forlornly at Millie.

'Vot a load of bunk! I do not know any other musical directors who have to put up vith such blatantly stupid interference vith their vork.' Grizelda grunted in exasperation. 'Sasha, get back over here! Ve had better have this track laid down in the next ten minutes or that vill be the end of me. And, for once, could you open your mouth and try to sing like a human being and not an alien making first contact?'

Sasha took a deep breath. 'I'll try,' he squeaked.

Millie gave him a pat on the back. 'You'll be great. Believe in yourself.'

Blade walked away from Caprice and sat down. So much for this being his big break.

Emmy looked at her watch. 'Oh goodness, I'd better check that the others are back in hair and make-up,' she said.

'Do Millie and I need to go as well?' Alice-Miranda asked.

'Can we stay for Sasha?' Millie added.

Emmy nodded. 'Sure, it won't take long to get you ready and, besides, we can't start without those three.' She smiled at Alice-Miranda and Millie. 'Thanks for being so kind to Sasha. He's a good kid.'

'Yeah, I really like him,' Millie said, the words falling out of her mouth before she had time to think about how they sounded.

Alice-Miranda giggled and nudged her friend. 'Oh?'

Millie recoiled. 'Not like that! You know what I mean. He doesn't have many friends and he deserves better than the way he's being treated by

Frau Furtwangler,' the girl blathered. She told herself to be quiet, but the words kept flowing like a bout of verbal diarrhoea. 'He's sweet and I think his parents have way too high expectations of him and, you know, I don't even think he wants to be a movie star.'

'It's okay, Millie. I like him a lot too,' Alice-Miranda teased. 'Come on, we'd better sit down before Grizzie loses her mind.'

Chapter 23

Sasha's final recording session had only been marginally better than his others, leaving Frau Furtwangler wondering how she was ever going to use him on the soundtrack. Grizelda couldn't believe that Eli Goldberg and his glittery wife and stupid mother would risk the entire production for the sake of that boy. Given the lad didn't much care about it either, there had to be another way. This was her show, after all.

Blade Crawford had been thinking the exact same thing, although his mother would be furious if he wasn't paid for the lead singing role. At the risk of being eaten alive, he decided to speak with Frau Furtwangler to see if there was anything he could do to help. Sasha noticed the pair of them together and sidled over to see what they were talking about.

Fortunately, the rest of the afternoon went far more smoothly than anything the children had been involved in so far. Andreas King seemed to step up his game, despite spending an awful lot of time whispering to the man with the clapperboard, who had a permanent look of bewilderment on his face. They got through the scenes fairly quickly and were able to reshoot a couple of things that he wasn't happy with from the day before.

Alice-Miranda didn't have a chance to speak to her uncle again. Lawrence was staying late with Alexa and the adult actors whose schedule had them shooting well into the night. They also had to fit in a recording session because they were due to head out on location the day after tomorrow.

At least the frost had begun to thaw between Caprice and Jacinta. Millie had threatened to knock their heads together if they didn't stop fighting and, thankfully, on the car trip home Bob had blasted the music and initiated a singalong, which kept them all entertained and put a halt to any squabbling. Caprice was so tired she was almost asleep in the back seat for most of the way.

That night Venetia Baldini was on location at some fancy LA restaurant, recording a segment for her television special, and Charlotte was out at a charity gala, leaving Magdalena in charge at home. But she wasn't there alone. Sigrid, Charlotte and Lawrence's personal assistant, was on hand to help with the babies until they were in bed.

Magdalena looked up from the huge frypan of onions that were sizzling on the stovetop as the seven children traipsed into the family room. '*Hola* my little superstars,' she trilled.

'Hola,' the group replied with varying levels of enthusiasm.

'I hope you're hungry,' the woman said, as she alternated between swirling diced onions in the frypan and expertly slicing celery stalks on the chopping board.

Caprice dropped her bag on the floor and slumped onto a stool at the island bench. 'I'm exhausted,' she moaned. 'Being a movie star is hard work.'

'Oh, my poor baby.' Magdalena cast an exaggerated frown in Caprice's direction. 'Imagine all those adoring publics and the big fat pay packets. It must be so terrible.'

Millie and Sloane giggled.

Caprice poked out her tongue. 'You're all mean.'

'Miss Caprice, you know I am only kidding. Mr Lawrence works his fingers to the bone and the things he must put his body through – it is hard to watch.' Magdalena shook her head. 'He was so fat for that last movie and then he must spend hours in the gym with that slavedriver Fabrizio so he can be back to his beautiful self. There was no candy for months, although perhaps Fabrizio was some candy for my eyes.'

The children chortled with laughter.

'Magdalena!' Millie gasped, pulling a face. 'You can't say that!'

'Oops!' The woman jiggled her hips and gave a cheeky wink. 'But I just did.'

'I'm starving,' Lucas said, heading for the pantry, where he located a box of his favourite cookies.

Magdalena clucked and shook her head. 'Oh, Master Lucas, at least eat the home-made chocolate-chip ones I have poured my sweat and tears into – but only one. Dinner will be ready soon and then it will be an early night for all of you.'

Lucas grinned. 'You just want to get rid of us so you can watch *The Glitzy Housekeepers of Bel-Air*.'

Magdalena's jaw dropped. 'No way! That show is rubbish.'

'You watch it all the time,' Lucas said, his eyes glinting. 'I've seen you.'

'Maybe, but only because I know three women on it and, boy oh boy, I am very lucky to work for your parents, mhmm,' Magdalena said, nodding to the onions.

Lucas reached for a second cookie, but was impeded by the flick of Magdalena's tea towel.

'Stop looking at me like that,' Magdalena scolded, unable to wipe the smile from her face. 'You are getting to be as bad as your father. Too charming for your own good. I will not take the responsibility when you are busting out of your pants with a belly like Eli Goldberg.'

'Well, you don't want to be as skinny or red as Sasha either,' Caprice said nastily.

'Leave him alone,' Millie snapped.

'Why? He's a terrible actor and an even worse singer,' Caprice retorted. 'He's going to wreck the whole movie.'

Alice-Miranda placed a glass of water in front of each of her friends and another for Magdalena over by the stove. 'Caprice, he's trying his best.'

'I think Sasha is lonely,' Millie said.

'Yeah, he's a good kid,' Jacinta added.

Caprice's eyelids flickered and she smirked. 'Do you like him, Millie? Or maybe Jacinta does? Oh, Lucas,' she said, pouting, 'you might need to find a new girlfriend. I know someone who could be persuaded.'

The boy almost choked. Surely Caprice was only saying that because she knew it would rile Jacinta.

Caprice began to laugh. 'Ooh, I see what's going on. Millie's got a crush on Sasha.' She started singing, 'Millie and Sasha sitting in a tree, K-I-S-S-I-N-G.'

'Stop it, Caprice!' Millie slammed her empty glass on the countertop. 'Why do you always have to be so horrible?'

'Yeah, what's wrong with you?' Jacinta seethed.

Sloane and Sep watched on in silence, shaking their heads.

'I think everyone should settle down,' Alice-Miranda said. She noticed Magdalena's face getting redder and it wasn't from the steam in the kitchen.

The woman turned from the cooking pot where the bolognaise sauce was now simmering away. 'Please, girls, I do not want any fighting. It has been bad enough with the twins this afternoon squabbling like seagulls. I cannot take anymore.'

'Sorry, Magdalena,' Millie and Jacinta chorused, both throwing one last glare at Caprice.

'Thank you, Miss Millie and Miss Jacinta. Now, what do you say, Miss Caprice? Are you going to play nicely or do you want to eat all on your own in the guesthouse?'

'Fine!' Caprice grouched. 'I'll be nice, but they have to be nice to me too.'

'Well, I'm sure that's entirely doable,' Alice-Miranda said. 'Why don't we all set the table and leave Magdalena to get on with dinner?' the girl suggested, garnering a grateful smile from the cook.

Sloane hopped up and located some placemats while her brother found the cutlery. Between the Sykeses, Millie, Alice-Miranda, Jacinta and Lucas, the children had the table set in no time. Caprice, on the other hand, didn't lift a finger or move from her perch.

'How was it at the theme park today?' Alice-Miranda asked, as she checked the place settings then went back to the sideboard for a couple of butter knives.

'Amazing,' Jacinta replied. 'We went on five rides – two of them were outdoor roller-coasters and the other three were indoors and had lots of CGI. I was almost sick on one of them. It felt as if we were being dropped right off the edge of a cliff but my stomach stayed behind.'

'Hopefully, we'll get to go again,' Lucas said. 'There are loads more rides we didn't try.' He folded an extra napkin and put it back into one of the kitchen drawers.

'It's a pity you two didn't get to come,' Sloane said.

Millie's eyes lit up, remembering her earlier escapade with Alice-Miranda. 'Well, we had heaps more excitement and drama when –'

Alice-Miranda placed her hand on Millie's arm and almost imperceptibly shook her head. 'It's probably best we keep that to ourselves until we talk to Uncle Lawrence,' she whispered. Millie's mouth formed a perfect 'O'.

'Why? What did you do?' Caprice asked, eyeing them suspiciously.

'Nothing,' Millie said quickly. 'I was making it

up so you'd feel better about forcing Alice-Miranda to stay with you.'

'No need. I didn't feel bad in the first place,' Caprice said, stretching back on the stool she hadn't moved from since they'd arrived home. 'And I certainly didn't twist her arm.'

Tyger Lombardi had turned her apartment upside down and still she couldn't find any books that didn't belong to her. She'd searched through her handbags and old camera bags. Whatever the thug thought she had, he was clearly mistaken, but that wasn't going to help when he called to make the exchange. She desperately needed her camera back. While the old SLR would suffice for now, she wanted those pictures of Ethan Kane. They were worth a lot of money and she could certainly do with topping up her bank account. If the moron had half a brain, he might even try to sell them himself, which would be a disaster.

Tyger needed to find this thug and see if he could be more specific. A book title would help.

She thought about taking a drive. The guy

clearly worked for someone rich with something to hide. Tyger sighed and shook her head. What was she thinking? Rich and with something to hide accounted for about half the population of this town. She'd have to wait until he made contact and hope that in the meantime she found what he was looking for.

Chapter 24

Alice-Miranda thought she was dreaming when she heard her aunt's voice and felt a hand on her shoulder.

'Sweetheart, I need you to wake up,' Charlotte whispered.

The girl roused from her slumber and realised it wasn't a dream at all. She rolled over and rubbed her eyes, trying to focus in the dim light. 'Is it time to get up already?' Alice-Miranda's words were wrapped around a yawn. She pushed herself against the pillows and saw that her aunt was dressed in a beautiful peacock-blue gown – ready for a party, not for bed. 'Is something the matter?' she asked, suddenly wide awake.

'I need to get to the hospital and I couldn't wake Magdalena no matter how hard I tried,' Charlotte replied. 'Lawrence has been involved in an accident on set. I'm not sure exactly what's happened, but he's been taken to Cedars-Sinai.'

Alice-Miranda blinked as the words sunk in. She nodded, trying to put on a brave face. 'Millie and I can listen for the twins and if we need anything I'm sure Venetia can help.' Alice-Miranda's eyes fell on the clock. It was just after eleven and, by the looks of it, her aunt had not long arrived home from the gala she'd been attending.

Charlotte leaned forward and hugged Alice-Miranda, her voice catching in her throat. 'Thank you, darling.'

The child smiled at her aunt and took the portable baby monitor. 'Uncle Lawrence will be fine. You know he will. He's completely bulletproof.'

Charlotte stood up. Her cheeks were drained of colour and she looked as if she were holding back tears. 'Of course. I'll call as soon as I know anything.' She gave Alice-Miranda a quick kiss on the top of her head and disappeared from the room.

Alice-Miranda stretched her arms and did her best to banish any terrible thoughts from her head. By now Millie had woken up too.

'Was Charlotte in here?' the girl asked sleepily.

Alice-Miranda switched on the lamp beside her bed and lay down on her side to face Millie. 'There's been an accident at the studio and Uncle Lawrence has been taken to hospital.'

Millie was out of bed like a shot. 'What happened?' she demanded.

'Aunt Charlotte doesn't know yet, but she's gone to be with him. We're watching the twins in case they wake up,' Alice-Miranda said, gesturing to the baby monitor on the bedside table.

Millie nodded. 'Do you want to go and get something to drink?'

Alice-Miranda followed her friend out onto the landing, where they ran into Lucas and Sep, who had woken too.

'What are you doing up?' Lucas asked.

Another door opened further along the corridor and Jacinta and Sloane emerged.

'What's going on?' Sloane asked, pulling her dressing-gown over her shoulders.

'Come on, we'll tell you over a cup of hot chocolate,' Alice-Miranda said, and the six friends padded down the stairs and into the kitchen.

Lucas switched on the television above the fire-place in the family room and flicked through the channels until he found a twenty-four-hour news station. Alice-Miranda had located a saucepan and had immediately set about making hot chocolate for everyone. There was no way any of the children were going back to sleep until they knew Lawrence was okay.

The bulletin was full of politics and several worrying stories, but there was nothing about any accident at Goldberg Studios.

'Dad probably tripped over something – you know how clumsy he can be,' Lucas said. 'It can't be that serious.' His stomach twisted as he said it, desperately wanting that to be the truth.

Down the hall, a light flicked on and Magda-lena shuffled out from her suite of rooms which occupied a small wing of the ground floor. Her hair was done up in rollers and an eye mask was pushed up on top of her head. She wore a fluffy pink robe and matching fluffy slippers.

'What are you all doing up at this hour?' the woman tutted. She fished about in her dressing-gown pocket and popped her reading glasses onto the tip of her nose. The clock on the kitchen wall indicated that it was just after midnight.

'Sorry to wake you, Magdalena,' Alice-Miranda said apologetically. 'I was trying to be quiet.'

'No, no. My sleeping is terrible these days. I sleep like a stone for the first hour, then I am awake and twiddling my thumbs until dawn. But what about you?' Magdalena clutched her cheeks in horror. 'Oh my goodness! I did not feed you enough for dinner!' She hurried over to the fridge to see what she could rustle up.

'Oh, it isn't that,' Alice-Miranda said. She bit her lip, uncertain of how to break the news gently. Magdalena was sure to be very upset. 'There's no need to be alarmed, but Uncle Lawrence has had an accident on set and Aunt Charlotte has gone to the hospital.'

The woman's face crumpled. 'No! What sort of accident? Is he all right? Oh my God in heaven above, he is dead!'

Lucas guided Magdalena towards one of the lounge chairs. 'He's alive, but we don't know what happened and Charlotte said that she would phone as soon as she had any news. It's probably nothing – knowing Dad, he's fallen over his own feet or something like that.'

The telephone on the bench rang and Alice-Miranda flew to pick it up. She nodded and hmmed several times. 'I'll let everyone know. See you soon, and give Uncle Lawrence a big hug from all of us,' she said before hanging up.

'Well?' Magdalena said, wringing her eye mask. 'Don't keep us suspending.'

The others looked at the tiny girl expectantly.

'Uncle Lawrence was shot,' Alice-Miranda announced. There was a gasp and Magdalena burst into tears. 'But the bullet was made of rubber, although the gun was meant to contain blanks. It was fortunate that it glanced off a railing before it hit his arm. It's only a flesh wound. He's going to have a big bruise, but other than that he's fine.'

'Oh, thank the Lord!' Magdalena pressed her palms together before crossing herself. She stopped crying and jumped up. 'I will make warm milk for when they get home. And all of you must go back to bed. You have another early call in the morning.'

But none of the children moved.

'No,' Lucas said. 'I want to see Dad.'

'I couldn't possibly sleep until I knew for sure that Lawrence was okay,' Jacinta said, and the rest of the children agreed.

Fortunately, it was only another hour before Lawrence and Charlotte walked through the back door. Lawrence's arm was in a sling and he was still wearing his clothes from the set. They looked an odd couple, the gunslinger and the beauty dressed for a gala.

Alice-Miranda made a beeline for the pair, launching herself at her uncle's middle, with Lucas hot on her heels. 'Thank goodness you're all right,' she murmured.

'Oh, Mister Lawrence, you had us so worried,' Magdalena blubbered. 'I was almost attacking in my heart.'

Clearly, Magdalena wasn't the only one who'd had a fright. Lawrence looked positively wrung out. 'I'm sorry. It was the silliest thing. Goodness only knows how it happened, but I hope that whoever is in charge of the munitions for the rest of the shoot gets it right. It was a bit of a shock when it hit me,' the man explained. 'Blasted thing stung worse than a wasp.'

'It's the curse!' Millie blurted, her eyes wide. She turned to face Alice-Miranda. 'Didn't Jerome say something about the curse of Nellie Williams? Don't forget there was Caprice's accident the other day and the disaster with our make-up.'

'He did mention it, but you know I don't believe in curses,' the child said. 'There has to be a rational explanation.'

Charlotte stood beside her husband, clutching his good arm as if she never wanted to let him go.

'I have warm milk and your favourite cookies,' Magdalena said, hurrying back to the kitchen. As she busied herself with a raft of midnight snacks, Lawrence sat down and regaled his family and friends with the whole startling affair, starting right from the beginning.

Chapter 25

The next morning, Lawrence Ridley's brush with death was all over the news. Someone, most likely at the hospital, had leaked the story and the headlines were sensational. 'Movie star's dice with death' the *LA Times* banner cried. 'Lawrence Ridley shot – accident or not?' read the headline of the *Los Angeles Daily News*. And that was only the print media. The television news was having a field day with a story about one of the world's best-loved movie stars being shot on set. The movie itself was a heavily guarded secret and, despite speculation about what it was, none of the media outlets had got that part right.

Abe Goldberg was on the doorstep at the Ridley-Highton-Smith mansion at seven o'clock, anxious to see how his leading man was faring. Most of the children were still fast asleep. Their call time had been pushed back until half past nine while a full investigation was being conducted on the sound stage and in the props department. Alice-Miranda was the first one up other than Lawrence and Magdalena. She got dressed and tiptoed downstairs, leaving Millie sleeping. The kitchen was a hive of activity with an apron-clad Magdalena up to her elbows in flour, having already prepared a special treat for her boss and his guest and with a second batch underway for the rest of the household.

Alice-Miranda was tasked with delivering a tray to the study, where the two men were talking. She poked her head inside the open door. 'Excuse me, Uncle Lawrence,' she said. 'Magdalena has baked something special for you and Mr Goldberg.'

'Good morning, sweetheart.' Lawrence grinned. 'Oh dear, Magdalena must really be fretting. She only ever makes home-made conchas on special occasions and it's nobody's birthday.'

Alice-Miranda trotted over to the desk and placed the tray beside her uncle. His arm was still in a sling, but apart from that he didn't look any different to usual, which she found heartening. 'Good morning, Mr Goldberg,' the child said, smiling.

'Morning, little lady. I imagine you had quite the fright last night,' the man said. Even at this early hour he was nattily dressed in a pinstriped suit, ready to head over to the studio.

'It's not every day your uncle is accidentally shot on the set of a movie,' Alice-Miranda replied. She turned to Lawrence, who was looking much more cheerful this morning. 'How is your arm?'

'It's absolutely fine and I feel ridiculous having it in a sling. It's literally a graze – you've no doubt had much worse. Actually, you were in bad shape when you had your horse-riding accident last term. I'll be taking it off before I go to the studio,' Lawrence said.

'I'm so glad that you're okay. I must say that you had us all worried last night,' Alice-Miranda said.

Abe nodded gravely. 'I got the call and couldn't believe it. It was like deja vu.'

'Why do you say that, Mr Goldberg?' Alice-Miranda asked. She couldn't help but think of

Millie's theory that the film was plagued by a curse. 'Has someone been shot on set before?'

The man went quiet as a strange look came over his face. 'It's taken a long time to get this movie off the ground,' he said, then paused. 'I just don't know . . .'

Alice-Miranda and her uncle both looked at him quizzically. 'What don't you know, Abe?' Lawrence asked.

'Oh, it's nothing.' Mr Goldberg closed his eyes tightly for a second. 'And in answer to your question, Alice-Miranda, there's been a few accidents over the years. People don't really believe that the movie-making business can be dangerous, but sadly that's not quite true.' He turned to Lawrence. 'I can't tell you again how sorry I am. Rest assured there will be a full investigation and, if I find any evidence of foul play, I won't stop until whoever was responsible has been dealt with,' the older man pledged. He stood up to leave. 'Don't you worry about coming in today. We'll reschedule things.'

Lawrence shook his head. 'Honestly, I'm fine and I know that this shoot is tight. We've got to have everything done before we head to the canyon tomorrow. I'll be there with the kids at half nine.' He hopped up to walk Abe to the door.

'Are we still having dinner with you and your family tonight, Mr Goldberg?' Alice-Miranda asked. She knew that her aunt had arranged it for this evening and she'd been looking forward to it all week.

'I hope so,' the man said. 'If I know my wife, it will be going ahead come hell or high water and I can promise you we will be right on time. That woman is never late for anything.'

'I'm looking forward to meeting her properly,' the tiny child said. 'She was at the studio yesterday with your daughter-in-law, but I didn't get to say hello.'

'She didn't tell me that.' Abe's eyebrows furrowed. 'I can't remember the last time Dinah dropped by. Between you and me, she's not a big fan of the place.'

Alice-Miranda wondered why that was the case. Goldberg Studios was a dreamland for so many people. 'It will be good to have a chat with her tonight and it will be lovely to spend more time with Sasha.'

Abe leaned down, closer to Alice-Miranda. 'Between you and me, how is that grandson of mine really doing?'

'He's trying hard, Mr Goldberg, and I think he's going quite well – he knows the script inside out,' the child said.

Abe exhaled. 'The casting agency said that he was the right kid for the job, but I'm afraid I have my reservations,' he confessed. 'Don't get me wrong, I love my grandson and he's a good boy, but I wouldn't have thought he was star material. That young fellow Blade, on the other hand . . . That kid has it all. I guess we'll have to trust that things are happening the right way around. My son says that he knows best.'

Alice-Miranda smiled at the man. She was about to speak when she hesitated.

'Is there anything else you'd like to tell me?' Abe Goldberg may have been advanced in years but his mind was still as sharp as a tack.

'Yesterday Millie and I went with Mr Lipp to fetch something for Frau Furtwangler from her bungalow,' the child began. 'Mr Lipp headed back before us, and while we were in the bathroom, two men came into the house. They were talking about where to hide something and were saying awful things about Tyger Lombardi. I was going to tell you yesterday, Uncle Lawrence, but you were so busy that I didn't get a chance.'

Lawrence and Abe looked at each other and both men raised their eyebrows.

'Tyger Lombardi doesn't have a very good reputation in this town. Whatever they were saying, I imagine she probably deserved it,' Lawrence said.

Alice-Miranda frowned. 'One of the men said that if she didn't give them what they were after, his boss had told him to make her disappear – permanently.'

'Do you think he was joking?' Lawrence asked.

Alice-Miranda shook her head. 'I saw the same man outside Grauman's Chinese Theatre the afternoon that I saw her too. She was taking pictures of us and then she looked over my shoulder and, from the colour of her face, I thought she must have seen a ghost – or maybe an assassin, as it's turned out to be.'

'What did he look like?' Abe asked. Alice-Miranda described the fellow, but Mr Goldberg drew a blank. 'It could be anyone. There are so many bodyguards and other people hanging around on the lot. He could have been working for one of the actors. Who knows? Heck, he could even be working for me and I wouldn't know it.'

'I'm worried about Miss Lombardi,' Alice-Miranda said. 'I know she's behaved unethically at times, but I don't think she likes her job very much. When she and I spoke, it sounded to me as though it was more about earning a living than enjoying invading people's privacy.'

'I'll talk to security and make sure that anyone matching that description is thoroughly checked out,' Abe said. 'There are cameras all over the lot, so I'll see if I can get some footage of the bungalow.'

'Did the two men see you and Millie?' Lawrence asked, realising that his niece and her friend could be in danger too.

'No,' Alice-Miranda said. 'When we realised what they were saying, we hid in the bathroom until they left.'

'What did they leave behind?' Lawrence asked.

'Nothing. They were in the wrong place – they thought it was bungalow number three but it was number one,' the child explained.

Abe Goldberg rolled his eyes. 'That old numbering system messes everyone up but I can't change it. My grandfather who started the studio decreed it in his will, would you believe? Of all the things he could have cared about, the random numbering of bungalows was important for some reason.'

'Do you know if anyone was using bungalow three yesterday?' Alice-Miranda asked.

Abe thought for a moment. 'No, but I can find

out and we can have the place searched. I'd better be going or my son will have me pensioned off and that's not happening as long as there is breath in this body. We'll see you all this evening and, Lawrence, please don't overdo it today.'

Lawrence and Alice-Miranda walked Abe to the back door. The man gave a wave as he headed across the garden to the back gate that led to the Goldberg Estate.

Alice-Miranda leaned in against her uncle and he wrapped his good arm around the girl's shoulders. 'Mr Goldberg seems such a kind man.'

'He certainly is,' Lawrence said. 'Now, what about we go and get some breakfast or we'll be in trouble with the boss.'

Alice-Miranda looked up at him and grinned. 'Yes, Magdalena won't be happy if you don't eat her conchas and they do smell delicious.'

It sounded as if the rest of the household was now up and about. Feet thudded in the hallway, followed by Magdalena's clarion call. '*Hola chicas!* I have especial treats for everyone.'

Chapter 26

Tish Crawford was pouring her second cup of coffee when the front doorbell rang. She would have asked Blade to answer it, only she'd just heard the hammer of the water pipes and the hiss of the shower. The condo was so small there was no such thing as privacy.

'Coming,' she called, unlatching the four locks. She opened the front door to find there was no one there. Tish looked out at the block but couldn't see a single soul. She stepped onto the porch and realised there was something bulging under the doormat. Tish peeled it back and pulled out a plastic shopping bag. She peered inside and gasped, her heart thumping. Her first thought was that it had been delivered to the wrong apartment and, if that were the case, she needed to find whoever owned it and soon, before it got her into a whole mess of trouble.

Tish looked around again, wondering if there was anyone spying on her from a hiding spot, ready to pounce if she took it, but there was no one – at least no one obvious. She hurried inside and closed the door, her fingers trembling as she snapped all four latches and drew the chain across too. She raced to the kitchen, where she lowered the blinds on the window above the sink, then dumped the contents of the bag onto the table.

There was a letter. Her name was typed on the front of the envelope. She could barely open it she was shaking so much. When she slid her finger under the flap and pulled out the page, there was a brief message – somewhat cryptic in its content, nonetheless she got the gist.

Stop interfering. Your son will have his day. Leave things alone and you can keep the cash. Tell anyone and the money will disappear.

It wasn't signed and there was no indication of where it had come from.

Tish stared at the bundle of banknotes. It was more money than she had ever seen and, boy, would it go a long way to covering some of their debts right now. She heard the water stop and shoved the cash back into the plastic bag, then into the freezer, stuffing the letter into the back pocket of her jeans. Tish closed the freezer door and leaned against the sink, her mind racing. A few minutes later, Blade walked into the kitchen and poured himself a bowl of cereal.

'You know, Mum, I think Frau Furtwangler is going to let me sing with Caprice on the soundtrack,' Blade said, between bites of his breakfast. 'And Andreas was talking about reshooting Sasha's scenes with me this afternoon. He thinks the kid's hopeless too.'

'Oh, really?' Tish sipped her tepid coffee. 'Honey, maybe you should back off a bit and give Sasha a chance.'

Blade looked at his mother. 'What are you talking about? You said I should do everything possible to get myself the lead. Sasha doesn't even want it. He was the one who suggested that they use my voice instead, and yesterday he said that he thought I'd make a much better lead than him.'

'But his parents have their hearts set on him being the star,' Tish said. She placed her mug in the sink and began pottering around.

'So what? You didn't seem to care about that yesterday when I could practically see the dollar signs in your eyes.' Blade frowned. He couldn't believe what he was hearing.

Tish grabbed a black cardigan off the back of a chair and threw it around her shoulders. 'You saw how upset the Goldbergs were about that,' she said.

'Yes, but you didn't hear what Frau Furtwangler and Andreas King said after you all left.'

Tish sighed. She knew that if she said anything more, her son would get suspicious. She needed to find out whatever she could about where that money had come from. A car pulled up in the driveway – Tish could see the black SUV through the edge of the ill-fitting blinds. 'Hurry up and finish your breakfast, then go and brush your teeth,' she said. 'Donny's here.'

At least Blade's part was big enough to warrant daily pick-ups – anytime Tish could leave her ancient sedan in the driveway and avoid the LA traffic was fine with her.

Blade pushed the bowl away and stood up. 'You know, Mum, sometimes I really don't get you,' he said, and stormed off to the bathroom.

Chapter 27

The studio gates were surrounded by fans, photographers and television crews trying to get a glimpse of Lawrence Ridley. To say that the world had gone into meltdown over his brush with death was something of an understatement. Abe Goldberg had barely managed to make it through himself, despite having his chief of security and head gatekeeper, Dylan, organise extra patrols before dawn. Dylan had a friend in the local police department who had arranged for a couple of cars to be stationed by the gates in case any of the paps got carried away.

Fortunately, window tinting was a standard accessory for every vehicle that was arriving at the lot, so it was almost impossible to know who was inside. Bob Loy engaged two decoys to throw the paps off the trail from the Ridley-Highton-Smith residence in Beverly Hills. Lawrence and the children ended up having something of an easy run of it, at least until they turned into the studio driveway and were confronted with the chaotic scene.

'You know what?' Lawrence said. 'I'm just going to get out and give them what they want, then they should leave me alone. The Goldbergs don't need this swarm out the front all day.'

'Do you think they'll go?' Millie asked, eyeing the excitable mob, some of whom were grown women holding posters of Lawrence and crying hysterically.

'If I give them all the same story, it's worth nothing. Sort of beats them at their own game, really,' Lawrence said with a wink.

Bob pulled up beside the gatehouse and he and Dylan had a quick chat before the gates opened and he drove on through. Instead of continuing up the winding driveway, Bob pulled over so Lawrence could hop out. As he walked towards them, the crowd at the gates went wild, calling his name and shouting questions as well as numerous declarations of love. A couple of women looked as if they'd fainted but soon picked themselves up and resumed their sobbing and screaming, much to the amusement of the children, who were watching from the car. Dylan opened the gates and accompanied Lawrence outside.

Alice-Miranda and the kids stayed put. The paps didn't know they were in the movie and it was probably best to leave it that way. Alice-Miranda craned her neck to see what was happening when she spotted Tyger Lombardi among the throng.

'Poor Dad,' Lucas said. 'Those journalists are completely nuts.'

Sep grimaced. 'I think those women are worse.'

But Lawrence Ridley decided there was only one way to handle things. 'Good morning, everyone,' he said, flashing them a winning smile. The crowd calmed with only the odd sob and gasp. 'I just want to say reports of my death last night have been widely exaggerated. There was an unfortunate accident while we were on set and I wound up with a very small and inconsequential wound from a rubber bullet that had been mistakenly loaded and fired instead of the blank we were anticipating. Thank you all for your concern and I would appreciate it if you could set the story straight. I'm fine and I am looking forward to getting back to work this morning. Thank you again for all your concern.' Lawrence gave them a wave with his good hand and turned to leave.

'Mr Ridley, what's the movie you're working on?' one veteran Hollywood reporter asked.

'Sorry, Gabe. I'm not at liberty to mention any details, but I'm sure that you will find out in due course. Now, if you'll excuse me, I need to get to work. Jerome won't be happy if I miss my make-up call,' Lawrence replied with a grin, and that seemed to satisfy the throng for the moment at least.

'Do you think someone's out to get you?' a small voice sang out.

Lawrence was surprised to find the voice belonged to, of all people, Tyger Lombardi and he was even more surprised to see that she was doing her best to keep out of sight. She was doing a great job of it, considering all eyes were now trained on her. While he resented the woman's constant intrusions into his personal life, he was concerned about what Alice-Miranda had told him that morning. 'Miss Lombardi, may I have a word?' he asked. She seemed taken aback to have been called by name and even more so to have been invited onto the hallowed studio land.

Dylan raised his eyebrows. 'Are you sure about this, sir?'

Lawrence nodded. 'I need to talk to her.'

As Tyger Lombardi entered the grounds, the other paps snapped dozens of pictures and the fans went wild. Lawrence knew that he was risking a slew of ridiculous stories about him and the woman, but if Alice-Miranda's instincts were correct, it sounded as though Tyger could be in some serious trouble. He would hate for something to happen to her and have done nothing to try to help.

'Miss Lombardi, I believe you met my niece a couple of days ago,' Lawrence said, as they walked into the guardhouse.

Tyger's shoulders slumped. 'Look, I hardly took any pictures of the kids.'

Several vehicles were now queued at the gate, but the crowd hadn't dispersed at all. Dylan interrupted the pair to suggest they move inside the lot, away from the gaze of the paps.

'Only if you're not going to tell me off,' Tyger huffed. 'It's been a bad week and, really, I don't need any more grief.'

'I've got no intention of telling you off,' Lawrence promised.

Dylan handed Tyger a visitor's pass on a lanyard and instructed her to wear it and be off the lot in half an hour or else he'd send someone to find her.

Bob Loy was out of the SUV as soon as he spotted his boss and the woman walking towards the vehicle. He opened the back door for Tyger. She flinched when she looked inside and saw the children. Millie was in the process of clambering over to the very back to sit with Lucas and Jacinta so there was enough space. Fortunately, the SUV had room for ten passengers plus the driver.

Alice-Miranda smiled at the woman and introduced her to everyone as Bob drove along the winding road to the sound stage. He pulled up in one of the designated parking spots. Lawrence instructed all the kids except Millie and Alice-Miranda to head to wardrobe and said he and the girls would be there shortly. The kids piled out of the car and Bob accompanied them to the building before returning and standing on the kerbside.

Lawrence swivelled around from the front. 'Miss Lombardi, yesterday Alice-Miranda and Millie overheard a couple of men talking about you here on the lot,' he began.

Tyger frowned. 'You know, what other people think of me is none of my business.'

'Well, that's a very sound philosophy to live by, but there's a bit more to it than that,' the man continued. Lawrence looked at his niece, who took up the rest of the story.

'One of the men was that fellow who was watching you outside Grauman's Chinese Theatre,' Alice-Miranda said.

'What?' Tyger swallowed hard. 'What was he doing here?'

'That we don't know, but he was with another man and they were going to hide something in one of the bungalows until they realised they were in the wrong place,' the girl explained.

'They thought they were in number three but they were really in number one,' Millie added. 'Because the numbers don't make any sense at all.'

'What else did they say?' Tyger's earlier lack of interest had now rotated one hundred and eighty degrees and she was desperate to hear more.

Alice-Miranda recounted how the fellow said that he would make her disappear – permanently.

Tyger shivered. She was also wondering exactly what that guy had been planning to hide in the bungalow. 'He says I've got a book that doesn't belong to me, but that's rubbish. I've turned my apartment upside down and my car too. It doesn't make any sense. He took my camera and he says that he'll give it back to me when I hand over what they want, but I'm going crazy trying to work out what that is.' Tyger began to shake and she looked like a woman who was at the end of her rope.

'When are you supposed to be making the exchange?' Alice-Miranda asked.

'Tonight,' Tyger said. 'So I guess this will be the last time I'll have the pleasure of chatting to you.'

Lawrence Ridley shook his head. 'No. We have to go to the police.'

'I'd rather not,' Tyger said. 'I'm on bail for trespassing, so my credibility is pretty much zero with the cops.'

'But you're in danger,' Millie said. 'Surely the police will do something about that.'

Tyger leaned forward, resting her head in her hands. 'This is Los Angeles. Everyone is in danger and I haven't disappeared yet, so I'm a bit of a non-story until then.'

'What can we do, Uncle Lawrence?' Alice-Miranda asked.

'Look, I don't expect you to do anything,' Tyger said. 'I can handle things. It's not the first time some beefed-up bozo has threatened me and I'm sure he was just showing off to his friend.'

But Alice-Miranda wasn't convinced.

'I'd better get out of here,' Tyger said, conscious that someone from security would come looking if she didn't leave soon.

'Bob will drive you back to your car,' Lawrence said, 'and I want you to have my number in case anything happens.' He scribbled it on a piece of paper and pressed it into her hand.

'Wow, imagine what I could get for this on the open market,' Tyger said with unreserved relish. She gazed at it a moment longer before realising the others were glaring at her. Tyger chuckled and held her palms in the air as if surrendering. 'I'm kidding!'

'Let me know what happens tonight,' Lawrence said.

'If I'm still alive, I will,' Tyger replied, although this time she was only half joking.

Lawrence and the girls hopped out of the car. He spoke to Bob for a minute and then the three of them walked over to the wardrobe department. Bob got back into the car and started the engine. He looked down and noticed that Lawrence's script was wedged between the centre console and the passenger seat. Bob instructed Tyger to wait for him while he delivered the script.

Tyger glanced around, thinking how disappointing it was to be on the lot but not able to explore it properly. Of course, she'd done the regular public back-lot tour, but once they'd discovered who she was and how powerful her camera lens was she'd been banned for life.

Tyger spotted a sign which got her attention. The bungalows. Didn't the little redhead say that the man had been looking for bungalow three when he was actually in bungalow one? She waited until Bob had disappeared inside the building before slipping out of the car. Doing her best to blend in, she walked across the road and turned left into the cul-de-sac. Tyger hurried along the street, scouting the numbers and hoping that three wasn't right at the end. Unless those thugs had a habit of stealing from innocent people, she had a hunch that when Alice-Miranda and Millie encountered them they were probably hiding her camera. If that was the case, wouldn't they get a nasty surprise when they returned to collect it before the exchange tonight? There would be no way to prove she'd taken it either. Once she had those pictures of Ethan Kane, she'd send them to her contacts and get out of town for a while. Then, by the time she came back, hopefully this mystery boss would have forgotten all about what it was they thought she had.

Chapter 28

After a spell in wardrobe, then hair and make-up, Alice-Miranda and Millie headed across to the sound stage to meet up with the other kids. Everywhere you looked there was something going on, from whip crackers practising their craft to caterers carrying towers of cupcakes. The gaffer and grips were checking the lighting and sound equipment while the on-set dresser was making sure that everything was in its rightful place, down to the last doorhandle.

Lucas was chatting with Sloane and Sep while the rest of their castmates for the scene were standing in huddles of two or three. Emmy was hovering nearby, waiting for their next instructions.

'Where's Sasha?' Millie asked.

'You mean your boyfriend?' Caprice teased.

Millie rolled her eyes. 'Whatever.'

'He's lost his voice,' Emmy said. 'I had a frantic call from his mother this morning saying she'd had the doctor to see him. Apparently, the man's administered some sort of miracle cure, but it might take a while to work.'

'Poor Sasha,' Alice-Miranda commented. 'I hope he'll still be able to come for dinner tonight.'

'I hope he'll still be able to do his part,' Millie said, looking concerned.

But that didn't seem likely. Andreas King was talking quietly with Blade, who was beaming from ear to ear and nodding. You could sense there was something exciting happening between them.

Millie gestured in the direction of the pair. 'Someone seems much happier today.'

'He's probably just landed Sasha's part,' Caprice said, glancing up from her script. 'And about time too. I mean, he's so full of himself, but he's way better at acting and singing than Sasha.'

'Oh dear. I think the Goldbergs will have plenty to say about that,' Alice-Miranda said.

'Well, if Sasha has lost his voice, I don't think they'll have a choice,' Caprice said, and flounced away to tell Wade there was a mistake in her script – several of her lines had been removed and that meant Blade or Sasha would have more to say than she did. That would be happening – over her dead body.

The set was a hive of activity with cameras and other equipment being moved into position. There were props attendants checking the set before a wagon train was pulled into place by four beautifully groomed horses.

'Look how well behaved they are.' Alice-Miranda pointed at the beasts standing patiently while some fellows made adjustments to the wagon. 'My Bony would go crazy with the noise and all those lights.'

'I hope the ponies we're going to be riding at the Grand Canyon are as calm as those guys,' Millie said. She watched the handlers patting their necks and cooing in their ears. There was another woman who was striding about and seemed to be in charge of them all.

'I can't believe we're going to be there tomorrow evening. It feels like a dream,' Alice-Miranda sighed.

'Or a nightmare if you're Sloane.' Millie pulled a face. 'I wonder if Sasha can ride?'

'It's going to be amazing,' Alice-Miranda added.

Millie nodded. 'Perhaps I should be an animal trainer for the movies when I grow up.' Just as the girl spoke, one of the horses lifted its tail and dropped a pile of steaming manure. An eye-watering stench filled the air. She grimaced as a young fellow quickly scooped up the mess. 'On second thoughts . . .'

Sasha walked into the building and spotted his castmates. Millie saw him too and gave the boy a wave.

'So you've lost your voice,' she said.

Sasha nodded.

'What's going to happen now then?' Alice-Miranda asked.

Sasha pointed at Blade, who looked to be reading over some lines then saying them aloud before diving back into the script.

'Your parents will be furious,' Millie said.

Sasha shrugged. 'It's for the best,' he whispered, 'and they won't even know if we don't tell them.'

Millie touched the boy gently on the arm. 'Don't try to talk.'

'Tea with honey sometimes helps,' Alice-Miranda suggested.

Millie eyed the catering station that was set up at the back of the building. 'I'm sure we can get some over there.'

Sasha smiled at her.

'Are you coming?' Millie asked Alice-Miranda.

'No, you go. I'll be over in a minute,' she said, distracted by Andreas King. The director was walking around the set scratching the back of his neck, then shuffling through a large stack of papers in a black folder. He sat in the director's chair and cradled his head in his hands.

Alice-Miranda decided she'd go and talk to the fellow. Andreas had made several rookie mistakes during the shoot, visibly losing confidence with each and every take. Alice-Miranda had put it down to nerves – that this was his big break, but right now she thought he looked as if he might cry.

She wandered over and plonked down in the chair beside him. 'Hello Mr King, is everything all right?'

He glanced at her. 'Man, I don't know. Maybe I've bitten off more than I can chew with this movie. I mean, I want it to be awesome, but I've got Abe on my case about Sasha – the kid's not that great, I'm afraid, and I think Blade would do a much better job. If I sack Sasha, Abe will kill me. But now the kid has laryngitis and we've got a deadline to meet.'

Alice-Miranda studied his face. Andreas seemed to have had a huge breakout of pimples on his chin since the beginning of the week and she could have sworn there were some grey hairs where before there were none.

'On top of that,' he continued, 'we almost killed Lawrence Ridley last night and, apparently, that's my fault, even though we have an armourer who's in charge of the firearms. Frau Furtwangler is ready to strangle me because I added some tracks to the music.' He shook his head despondently. 'The crew say the movie's cursed. I didn't believe it at first, but now I'm not so sure. Do you think that could be true?' He was certainly not the same cool customer who had strutted onto the set a few days ago.

'The mishap with Uncle Lawrence was an accident. He wasn't really hurt, thank goodness,' Alice-Miranda said. 'I think you're doing a great job.'

'I'm trying, but I'm pretty sure the crew hates me,' Andreas said.

'Perhaps if you stopped pretending that you knew everything and asked for help, they might respect you a little more. From what Uncle Lawrence has told us, this is a really experienced team,' Alice-Miranda said.

Andreas pouted. 'Yeah, but I've just come out of film school and I know all this new stuff and they're old and stuck in a time warp.'

An attitude like that, Alice-Miranda thought, wouldn't help him win the admiration of his colleagues. 'What did you mean about adding some tracks to the music?' Alice-Miranda asked. 'I'm not sure that you'd want to mess with Frau Furtwangler. She's a very passionate woman.'

A huge hullabaloo sounded from the other side of the studio.

'Vere is that idiot?' Frau Furtwangler's voice echoed around the building. 'I vill tear off his arms ven I get hold of him! He has ruined everything. How dare he add a beatbox track under my music. I hate this movie. I hate it so much that I quit!'

Mr Lipp chased after the woman, trying his best to placate her. 'Oh no, Frau Furtwangler, you can't do that. You're a genius. Your music is perfection. *You* are perfection!'

As the words flew out of his mouth, the entire building fell silent.

'Oops, poor Mr Lipp,' Millie said, watching his face turn from slightly pink to deep crimson.

'Vot did you just say?' Frau Furtwangler demanded.

'Nothing?' he squeaked.

'So, you have no backbone either. You say something and then take it back. Like Abe Goldberg, who said I was in charge of the music on this film and now he has given Andreas King control and the imbecile has mangled it with his adolescent ideas.' The woman was imposing on a good day, but right at that moment she seemed to have grown at least a foot taller and was ready to spiflicate anyone who came within three feet of her.

Mr Lipp pushed his shoulders back and stood his ground. 'No, Grizelda, I am not taking anything back. I said that your music was perfect and you're perfect too. I have never met anyone like you.'

Frau Furtwangler leaned in close to the man. He could smell her perfume – a dark musky scent that made his nostrils quiver.

'Mr Lipp, you know that most men are afraid of me. I vould bet my last dime that Andreas King is somevere in this building shaking in his high-top sneakers because he knows that ven I find that veasel vorm good-for-nothing, acne-ridden teenager, I vill crush him under my size fourteen shoes. But you – you are brave and you are kind and I think . . .'

The entire cast and crew were mesmerised by the bizarre declarations being made by the pair.

'. . . you are a man. A man who deserves my love.' Grizelda wrapped Mr Lipp in her arms, puckered up and kissed him smack on the lips.

A huge cheer erupted and the children and adults all clapped and whistled and stamped their feet. When Frau Furtwangler finally came up for air, Mr Lipp's face was the colour of the scarlet suit he was wearing.

Alice-Miranda looked around. It appeared that Andreas King had used the distraction to make his escape. She scanned the exits just in time to see him fleeing out the far door.

'Frau Furtwangler, why don't we go back to the studio and see if we can find a way to save the soundtrack?' Mr Lipp suggested.

'You are right, Harold,' the woman said, patting her curls. 'I am a genius and if anyone can salvage this project it is me.' She grabbed him by the arm and the pair walked out of the building with their heads held high.

'Mr Lipp was practically floating across the floor,' Jacinta giggled. She looked at Lucas, who slipped his hand into hers.

Caprice poked out her tongue. 'Oh, gross, don't you two get any ideas. That was enough smooching for one day.' She rolled her eyes as Alice-Miranda hurried back to the group.

'Where's Mr King?' Millie asked.

Alice-Miranda shrugged. 'It's complicated,' she said.

'Seems to be a bit of a theme around here,' the red-haired girl replied, waggling her eyebrows.

Chapter 29

The front doorbell rang at exactly half past six. Alice-Miranda and Millie were on official meet-and-greet duty while Lucas and Jacinta were out the back, helping to set up the tables on the terrace. Sloane and Sep were on kitchen duty with Magdalena while Caprice was still in the guesthouse preening.

It had been a long day on set, with Lawrence taking over directorial duties in addition to his acting role, following the sudden disappearance of Andreas King. Despite the best efforts of crew members to locate the man, he seemed to have vanished into thin air. Someone said there was a report of a young guy matching his description up at the theme park, riding the roller-coaster endlessly for hours. Creatives could be tricky at times and, while his absence had been reported to Eli Goldberg, the man didn't want to make too much of a fuss, lest Andreas King throw in the towel and leave them completely in the lurch. This movie was proving far more bothersome than even Eli had anticipated.

The children and Lawrence had arrived home to find Magdalena and Venetia with their sleeves rolled up standing side by side in the kitchen and cooking up a storm for this evening's party. Numbers had grown somewhat with Charlotte having invited the Crawfords and Mr Lipp and Frau Furtwangler.

Alice-Miranda opened the door. 'Hello Mr Goldberg, it's lovely to see you again. May I introduce my friend Millie?'

'Good evening to you both.' The skin around the old man's eyes crinkled as he smiled. 'And this is my wife, Dinah.'

'Oh, hello Mrs Goldberg. I'm sorry we didn't get to meet properly the other day at the studio.' Alice-Miranda offered her hand.

The woman was immaculately dressed in a smart pair of black trousers and a stunning silk blouse in a shimmering shade of gold. Her short grey hair was cut in a style that was grandmotherly but elegant.

'Oh, that's right, Alice-Miranda mentioned you were at the studio yesterday. You didn't tell me you were coming,' Abe said with a frown.

For a split second, Dinah Crawford seemed to cast Alice-Miranda something akin to a death stare, but it evaporated so quickly the child wondered if she'd imagined it.

'Aviva dragged me out with her new friend and insisted we stop by to see how the boys were doing,' Dinah said. 'You know I only went so she would stop nagging. If I had my way, we'd be on that cruise in the South Pacific.'

'You know I can't take any time away from the studio, especially not right now,' Abe said, patting his wife's hand.

'Well, I'll be dead in a box before you take me anywhere,' Dinah huffed, her voice taking on a harder edge.

'I'm so sorry, Mrs Goldberg, I didn't mean to tell tales,' Alice-Miranda apologised, aware that she seemed to have caused a bit of a feud. 'It was none of my business.'

'Alice-Miranda, don't be silly. This is Hollywood, sweetheart.' Mr Goldberg raised his caterpillar eyebrows. 'Everyone's business is everyone's business.'

'Not in our family, it isn't,' Dinah said.

'It is, according to the paparazzi,' Millie piped up.

'Ugh,' Dinah Goldberg sighed. 'Nothing but bloodsucking leeches making money from other people's miseries.'

'You don't always look unhappy in the pictures.' Abe Goldberg winked at Millie and Alice-Miranda, but it was clear that Mrs Goldberg was in no mood for jokes.

'There had better not be anyone lurking about here in the bushes tonight,' the woman said.

'You mean like a tiger up a tree,' Millie quipped.

Dinah's brow wrinkled. 'What tiger? What are you talking about?'

'Tyger Lombardi,' Millie said. 'She took photographs of Charlotte and the twins from the tree out the front of the house.'

'That woman. She needs to be stopped,' Dinah said. 'Could we go inside please, Abe? I need to make a call.'

Abe shrugged, wondering what was so urgent. Although, knowing his wife, Dinah probably needed to confirm a time with one of her charity committees or the like.

'I'll show you through,' Millie offered, hoping it wasn't something she'd said. But Caprice intercepted her just inside the hall.

'Good evening, Mr and Mrs Goldberg, it's such a pleasure to have you dining with us tonight,' the girl cooed. 'May I accompany you to join the other guests? I'd love to tell you all about what's been happening on set. It's been absolutely thrilling working on a Hollywood movie.'

Millie turned around and pretended to gag. Caprice was clearly trying to shore up her career prospects. Millie walked back out to join Alice-Miranda as another car pulled up to the entrance. A driver exited the vehicle and opened the back door of the limousine. Frau Furtwangler barrelled out, followed by Mr Lipp.

Alice-Miranda danced around on the front porch, delighted to see the new couple. Millie was doing her best not to giggle. The pair looked spectacular. Mr Lipp was positively radiant in a canary-yellow suit with a bright pink shirt and a spotted blue cravat. Frau Furtwangler's dress, covered in blue polka dots of the same hue as Mr Lipp's cravat, was the perfect complement.

Mr Lipp grinned at the girls, and Alice-Miranda thought he looked the happiest she'd ever seen him.

'Did you have a good day in the end?' she asked quietly.

'It's getting there,' he said, 'as long as Andreas King stays out of the way and lets Frau Furtwangler shine.'

'Harold, please, I am starving and I need a glass of champagne,' the woman crowed. 'You must find something for me right avay before I faint from hunger pains.'

Mr Lipp pouted at her. 'Of course, Zelda, my lovely.'

'Oh, Harry,' she said, touching the tip of his nose with her pointer finger, 'you are so cute, like a little puppy.'

Mr Lipp made some barking sounds, as if he were a Chihuahua, and the couple disintegrated into a fit of giggles. Alice-Miranda did her best not to join them. The loved-up pair linked arms and pranced out to join the other guests, guided by Millie, who was having a great deal of trouble biting her tongue to stop herself from laughing.

Chapter 30

Dinner was a huge success and had everyone clamouring for seconds, and in some cases thirds. After dessert, the children left the adults to their chatter on the terrace and headed inside. Magdalena was in the kitchen, on cloud nine as she stacked the dishwasher. Venetia had credited her with doing most of the work, garnering compliments from everyone (and even a very sneaky job offer from Aviva Goldberg, which Magdalena politely declined on the spot). While Alice-Miranda and Jacinta helped Charlotte give Marcus and Imogen their baths and put the babies to bed, the rest of the children were in the family room discussing what to do next.

'Have you got a games room here?' Blade asked Lucas.

'It's in the basement, but it's being renovated at the moment,' Lucas replied. 'We could watch a movie in the theatre room?'

Caprice rolled her eyes. 'I want a break from movies tonight.'

'What about you, Sasha?' Blade looked at the boy. 'I heard that you have a bowling alley and a half-sized basketball court and an old-fashioned pinball parlour as well as ten swimming pools.'

'I'm not sure Mum and Dad will want us to go there,' the boy croaked. His voice was beginning to return, but he still sounded like a frog. 'Anyway, that's at Grandma and Grandpa's place, not our house. And there are only three pools, not ten.'

'So, you've got all this really cool stuff, but you don't want to share. Doesn't take Einstein to work out why you don't have any friends,' Blade said, reclining in his chair and doing a very good job of appearing bored out of his mind.

'Why do you have to be so mean, Blade?' Millie

snapped. 'Like Sasha said, all those things are at his grandparents' place.'

'Defending your boyfriend again?' Caprice teased.

'Just put a sock in it, will you?' Millie bit back.

'Let's go then, Sasha,' Blade said, standing up.

'I have to check with Mum and Dad,' the boy whispered. He disappeared to speak to his mother, who barely registered the boy's presence let alone comprehended what he was asking. Aviva waved Sasha away, eager to continue her conversation with Venetia Baldini, who was recommending a couple of new restaurants she'd visited during the week.

Sasha mooched back to the others.

'Well, are we going or what?' Blade eyeballed the lad.

Sasha nodded, but didn't seem in a hurry to leave. He stood next to Millie, who got a feeling the boy wanted to tell her something.

'Come on then, what are we waiting for?' Blade made a move and the others followed.

Sasha led the group through Charlotte and Lawrence's extensive back garden to the ornate iron gate that accessed the rear of the Goldberg estate. The path on the other side immediately split into three.

'This way,' the boy said. He hoped that no one would get lost, although at least the place was well lit. Lampposts which his grandmother had imported from Paris lined the route, giving the garden an otherworldly ambience.

'Is it much further?' Caprice whined. She had a tiny blister on her little toe, but given the fuss she'd made about it at the studio, Emmy had been convinced she'd have to call the paramedics.

Millie was beginning to wonder if they were ever going to reach their destination. They seemed to have been walking for quite a long time. The children passed through a woodland and a rose garden laid out in a formal style as well as other smaller secret gardens along the way. Every part of the landscape was lit so that the delights of the Goldbergs' estate could even be witnessed at night. Finally, the path opened on to a vast terrace with a circular pool that was surrounded by high columns and a cabana that ran around almost half of it. It was the most glamorous thing Millie had ever seen. Like everything else, it too was illuminated.

'Wow!' she gasped, and her disbelief was echoed by the others. 'This is beautiful.'

Sasha hadn't really ever thought about it that much before. 'It is, isn't it?' he agreed.

Past the pool a huge house came into view. Neoclassical in style, and set over at least three storeys, possibly more, the structure wouldn't have looked out of place on a hillside in France or Italy.

Blade's eyes widened. So, this was what being a movie mogul bought you. His head had already been spinning when he and his mother had arrived at Lawrence Ridley's house. Compared to the fleapit condo they rented in the valley, it was hard to imagine living in such luxury. Now he had the lead, perhaps they could afford to move somewhere nicer. Blade had been surprised by his mother's reaction to the idea that he was probably going to take over Sasha's role, but Sasha had begged him to do it and Andreas was happy about it too. The trio had decided that they would keep things under wraps for now and, during the editing stage, Andreas would choose who he was going to use. Surely then Blade would be paid accordingly and by that stage it would be too late to change anything.

The children followed Sasha to the rear of the mansion. He hoped that he didn't run into Dolores, his grandparents' live-in housekeeper. Then he remembered Friday was ballroom-dancing night.

They walked into the house and through an enormous dark timber kitchen, before heading into a long hallway, where they made a left into a timber-panelled alcove. Sasha pushed a button on the wall and, to the group's surprise, an elevator bell pinged.

'Whoa, you have an elevator to go to the basement?' Sep's eyes were on stalks.

'Are there stairs too?' Millie asked.

Sasha nodded. 'Yes, but they're in a stupid place on the other side of the house. This is easier.'

'It's a bit creepy,' Jacinta whispered to Lucas, and the boy reached out and held her hand.

Caprice was standing behind the pair and wrinkled her lip, setting her face into a sneer. 'Hey, Lucas, I'm scared too. Can you hold my hand?' she quipped.

Jacinta turned and eyeballed the girl. 'Go away, Caprice.'

Fortunately, the lift arrived and Sasha pushed back the old-fashioned wire doors. The group piled inside.

There was a collective intake of breath as the children descended into the bowels of the mansion.

When Sasha slid the grilles back, they couldn't believe the size of the space and, true enough, there was a half-sized basketball court and at the other end of the vast room was a bowling alley with three lanes. There were electronic scoreboards and three seating areas. In addition to all that was the largest L-shaped lounge suite anyone had ever seen and a giant movie screen as well. In another corner was a miniature version of Patty's Diner from the studio lot, equipped with booths and a counter and even a kitchen.

'Your dad must have loved growing up here,' Alice-Miranda said.

Sasha shook his head. 'This wasn't here back then. My grandparents had it built for my big brother and sister when they were little. They thought it would be a way to get the grandchildren to visit more often. But they're both away at college now, so it's only me at home.'

'I wouldn't just be visiting,' Blade said, leaping onto the corner lounge and folding his arms behind his head. 'I'd never leave. This is awesome.'

Sasha grinned. 'I guess it's pretty cool.'

'Pretty cool?' Blade grimaced and jumped off the lounge to wander around. 'Would you like to swap?

I have a television with an extremely limited range of stations at my place.'

Sasha's smile grew wider. 'So, what do you want to do first?'

There was a vote for bowling, followed by basketball. With Millie and Alice-Miranda's help, Sasha began to organise some snacks from the diner, but they soon realised they were running low on almost everything. He'd have to pop up to his grandmother's overstocked pantry.

'This place is incredible,' Blade said, as he entered the children's names into the scoreboard.

'Thanks,' Sasha said. He wished the kids at school were as nice to him as everyone here was tonight.

'Okay, Sasha, you're up first,' Blade called.

'I'm hungry,' Caprice moaned. It was no wonder as she'd hardly touched her dinner, much to the annoyance of her mother.

'Millie and I can go upstairs and get some things,' Alice-Miranda offered. 'If the pantry's not too hard to find.'

Sasha danced around on his toes, clearly eager to go and play. Tonight, for the first time in forever, he actually felt like he might be making some proper friends. Even Blade seemed okay. Sasha knew he should accompany the girls, but the pantry was just off the kitchen and Dolores labelled everything right down to 'snacks for the playroom'. It would be easy to find. 'Are you sure you don't mind?' he asked.

'Of course not.' Alice-Miranda smiled at him. She had a feeling that being asked to play on Blade's bowling team meant a lot more to the boy than satisfying Caprice's hunger pains.

After some short instructions from Sasha, the girls hopped into the lift and pressed the button that would take them up to the ground floor. Except that something went wrong and the elevator didn't stop. The contraption kept going for at least two more floors and when it finally did come to a jolting halt, despite pressing the button again, the old beast refused to move. The doors opened to reveal a dimly lit hallway.

'Well, this is definitely not the kitchen level,' Millie said.

'No, it isn't,' Alice-Miranda agreed. 'Perhaps we should try the old-fashioned way. There must be a staircase around here somewhere.'

The girls wandered into the hallway, which soon split into three directions.

'You go that way and I'll see what's down there,' Millie said. 'Yell if you find it.'

Alice-Miranda felt certain there had to be a set of stairs somewhere close by. She walked to the end of the corridor, opening and closing doors to several bedrooms until one that housed an enormous study caught her eye. There was a lamp on in the corner, illuminating the pretty room which had a fireplace and overstuffed sofas as well as a huge mahogany desk. It reminded Alice-Miranda of her Granny Valentina's study, which was the perfect place to curl up with a book on a chilly day.

Alice-Miranda studied the spines on some of the books on the fitted bookshelves that took up one whole wall. Someone was clearly a fan of Agatha Christie. She spotted a title she remembered Miss Reedy having mentioned recently and couldn't resist pulling it down off the shelf. Alice-Miranda flipped open the cover and was surprised to find the pages had been glued together and the inside cut out. Concealed within was a smaller book. She snapped it shut and replaced it on the shelf, berating herself for snooping. Alice-Miranda hurried from the room and retraced her steps back to the place where she and Millie had split up, but her friend was nowhere to be seen.

Chapter 31

'Millie, where are you?' Alice-Miranda called in a voice no louder than a whisper. She felt a churning in her stomach, and even though she hadn't looked any further than spotting the book inside the book, it felt like prying. Alice-Miranda headed in the opposite direction, opening and closing more doors, but Millie seemed to have vanished into thin air. She reached the end of the hallway and opened the final door, which led to a staircase.

'Millie, are you up there?' Alice-Miranda called

again. Her voice sounded much louder as it echoed around the walls.

'You have to see this, Alice-Miranda,' Millie hissed back, much to her friend's great relief.

'What are you doing? We're supposed to be looking for a way back to the kitchen, not snooping about in the attic,' Alice-Miranda chided.

'I know but I couldn't help myself and this is incredible,' Millie replied.

Alice-Miranda dashed up the stairs, the horrible feeling in her stomach intensifying. She reached the landing and was speechless. Alice-Miranda had been expecting an attic in the rafters, but this was like a much smaller version of the costume department at Goldberg Studios with part of the props department thrown in for good measure. There were racks and racks of clothes as well as huge display cabinets containing all manner of movie memorabilia. It could have passed for a museum if it wasn't hidden at the top of the Goldbergs' mansion.

'Look at this.' Millie pointed at one of the display cases. There were labels on each item indicating which film they were from.

The girls marvelled at the costumes and props, everything from knights with swords to spacesuits and breathing apparatus. So many famous movies from the twentieth century and beyond were represented and there were photographs of the actors on set too.

'This must be from all the westerns the studio has made,' Millie said, as she scampered towards the end of the room. Alice-Miranda scurried over to join her. 'Look at all those hats and boots and the guns too.'

But there was much more than that. There were beautiful tortoiseshell combs and ribbons and handkerchiefs, bonnets and snuffboxes. Alice-Miranda was entranced by the trinkets and knick-knacks and couldn't imagine why they were locked away here in the top of the house.

'Hey,' Millie said, a frown creeping onto her forehead. 'Check out the name of the movie.'

'That's strange,' Alice-Miranda said. 'I didn't know we were doing a remake of an old film. From everything I'd heard, this was a new script and a new concept. Why do you think no one has said anything? We'll have to ask Uncle Lawrence.' She glimpsed a framed photograph of two actors dressed just like Lawrence and Alexa's characters. The resemblance was uncanny. 'Come on, we've got to get back – Caprice will be starving and Sasha will be wondering where we are.'

Alice-Miranda turned on her heel and Millie reluctantly followed.

The girls took the third hallway and soon located the home's magnificent central staircase. They hurried down two flights to the ground floor and tried to decide where the mysterious stairs to the basement might be. But they needn't have worried as Sasha emerged from the darkness.

'Sorry, your elevator seems to have gone haywire. It took us to the top of the house, then refused to budge. We got a bit lost,' Alice-Miranda said.

'So, you didn't find the pantry?' Sasha rasped, and the girls shook their heads. 'Never mind. Caprice discovered a cupboard full of chips and snacks downstairs that I'd missed.'

'We did stumble upon the most amazing museum,' Millie said excitedly. 'In the attic.'

Sasha gulped and for a second Alice-Miranda thought the boy was going to pass out right in front of them. 'No one's allowed to go up there,' he said, his voice trembling. 'It's Grandpa's special place.'

Millie scrunched up her face. 'Sorry, I found it by accident and I couldn't help taking a look.'

'Please don't tell anyone, especially not my grandparents. They'd be upset and we've got to get back. We're not even supposed to be here. I told my mum we were going to *our* place. She'll be mad if we're late and might even come looking – well, she'd call our housekeeper and then she'll know we were never there in the first place.'

Alice-Miranda felt doubly bad about their upstairs excursion. 'We didn't mean to do the wrong thing,' she said. 'Let's go and get the others.'

Sasha managed a tight smile. 'What's up there?' he asked.

Millie's eyebrows jumped up in surprise. 'Do you mean you've never been?'

The boy shook his head. 'The door is usually locked.'

Millie and Alice-Miranda shared a look and wondered why it was a secret.

Tyger Lombardi struggled awake. Her head was pounding and she breathed deeply through her nose. Her mouth was covered with something – tape, maybe – and her hands and feet were bound together with what felt like rough strands of rope. She was in a cupboard and there was an eye-watering smell of mothballs. At least she had her camera back. She could feel it beside her, although she had no idea if it was still in one piece. The last thing she could remember was finding the bag in the bungalow. It was hidden in the back of the wardrobe, just sitting there. And now her head was throbbing and she couldn't see properly.

She pressed her elbow against her jacket pocket and could hear the crinkling of the paper inside it. Lawrence Ridley's mobile number didn't seem to be quite the prize it had earlier. Surely someone had to come for her. They couldn't leave her there forever – and she was busting to go to the loo.

Tyger had been in a few scrapes before, but this . . . well, this seemed kind of serious.

Chapter 32

His heart thumped hard as he held the door open for his passenger, who slid into the back of the limousine. He closed the door and hopped into the driver's seat, glancing in the rear-vision mirror and wiping the beads of perspiration that peppered his brow.

'Do you have it?' the passenger demanded from the shadows of the back seat.

'No. She knows what she's got and, if you don't pay, she's going to the papers,' he said.

'I should have realised she'd do something like this. The paps are nothing but bloodsucking scum,' the person said. 'How much?'

The driver could feel his pulse rate rising. It felt good to be believed. 'Five million.'

'Five million! She can't be serious.'

'She has promised to disappear,' he added quickly. 'To drop off the face of the earth.'

'For that much, she'd better set up house on the moon. I still want it back.'

'It doesn't really matter, does it? If she knows what's inside, you just need to buy her silence,' he reasoned.

'And not know where it is or who else might find it? Without it there is no deal, and I don't want to hear from you until you have it.' The passenger raised the divider that separated the two of them and it remained that way for the rest of the journey.

Chapter 33

There was a buzz in the air as the group boarded their chartered flight to McCarran International Airport in Nevada. From there they would travel by coach to the camp site twenty miles from the West Rim of the Grand Canyon. Aviva Goldberg and Tish Crawford were allowed to come along too, but they were under strict instructions not to interfere. To be sure, Emmy had organised activities for them, and it was no accident that they took place a great distance from the set. Andreas King wasn't happy about them being there at all, but as things had been arranged prior to his appointment, he really didn't have a say. He seemed to have got over his sulk and was back working on the film, having sent a message apologising to Eli Goldberg, although in reality he seemed to be blaming pretty much everyone else for his woes. Eli was appalled, but Andreas wasn't the first petulant director he'd had to deal with and he surely wouldn't be the last.

So, apart from the ten child actors, there was Tish Crawford, Aviva Goldberg and Mr Lipp. Venetia Baldini was still in LA filming and Lawrence and Alexa were arriving later that evening as they were recording with Frau Furtwangler all day.

Emmy handed the children their scripts just before take-off and asked that they read them carefully. The location activities would include scenes outside the schoolhouse and a bit of riding, rounding up some buffalo as well as general shots in the town. The final scene involved a stampede, which sounded both thrilling and terrifying. Everyone had a stunt double and none of the children were expected to ride unless they were completely at ease. Millie and Alice-Miranda couldn't wait, but Sloane was still more than happy to leave that to the experts.

Apparently, there would be a lot more of the adult cast on set, as they were trying to knock over the location shots in two grabs – with the children and again in a couple of weeks' time. The crew who had been working on the sound stage had driven out on Friday night, but there had been a small army of people setting up for weeks now, with more buildings having been constructed and much of the sound stage town replicated in real life.

Alice-Miranda was sitting beside Millie and reflecting on what they'd seen in the Goldbergs' attic the night before.

'Why do you think Mr Goldberg keeps his collection a secret?' the girl asked, turning to her friend.

Millie shrugged. 'Who knows? People do seem a tad strange in Hollywood. Maybe he's planning to open a museum one day.'

'That's entirely possible,' Alice-Miranda conceded. 'I read somewhere that a very famous actress called Debbie Reynolds amassed a huge collection of movie memorabilia and wanted to have a permanent exhibition somewhere, but she ran out of money and space and then had to sell it all off. You'd think that Hollywood would have something like that already, wouldn't you?'

'Sasha looked as if he was going to faint when he realised we'd been up there. I'm glad he warned us, otherwise I'd have blurted all about it. I don't want to get him in trouble. The poor boy has enough problems,' Millie said. She was furiously flicking through the channels on the tiny television set located in the headrest of the seat in front of her.

Alice-Miranda buried her nose in her script for the rest of the journey, wanting to familiarise herself with her lines and the schedule.

The flight seemed to take no time at all and, before they knew it, the pilot announced their descent into the airport.

'Hey, is that Las Vegas over there?' Jacinta asked. She was looking out of the window as the plane was coming in to land.

'Yes, it is.' Aviva Goldberg nodded vigorously. 'Pity it's still daylight. There's nothing quite like the Las Vegas strip at night. And that fountain out the front of the Bellagio is a sight to behold.'

'That's true,' Alice-Miranda said. 'I came with Mummy and Daddy once when I was little and the fountain was my favourite thing. I wasn't very keen about the rest of it, though. Especially not inside the casinos, where people smoke and mostly lose lots of money.'

'They win too, you know,' Caprice said. 'I've seen it in movies.'

'But movies aren't real life,' Alice-Miranda said. 'I'd bet there are probably many more losers than winners. How do you think the casino bosses get to be so rich?'

'Like Felicity Fang's dad in Macau,' Millie piped up.

'Oh, please, don't mention her. She's the biggest brat I've ever met,' Caprice sniped, eliciting more than a few raised eyebrows from the others. 'You can all stop that right now. Don't think I didn't see. And you, Mr Lipp, I'd have thought better of you,' Caprice berated the man to a titter of giggles.

The plane landed and there was a flurry of activity as the children collected their things and hopped off, walking only a couple of metres to a waiting tour bus. It was black with tinted windows and seemed quite a bit more glamorous than the average coach. The trip to the camp site would take around four and a half hours providing they didn't make too many stops along the way.

'Can you believe this bus?' Sep said. He walked through the kitchenette in the middle of the vehicle to the lounge area at the back. There were ten rows of regular seats at the front as well.

'Wait until you see the trailers you'll be staying in,' Emmy said with a grin.

Caprice baulked. 'A trailer! Isn't there a hotel out there?'

'I think you'll find that the trailer will be far better than any of the motels we see on the way,' Emmy said. She winked at Alice-Miranda, who giggled. The girl was well aware that the trailer Emmy was alluding to was a luxury motorhome that would put most apartments to shame. Uncle Lawrence had told them all about the beast he'd had on location in the Rocky Mountains a while back and it sounded amazing.

'It had better be,' Caprice snapped.

Blade was sitting in front of the girl and leaned around to speak to her. 'Do you want to go over our lines together?' he asked tentatively.

'Okay.' Caprice shrugged. 'But I know them already.'

Alice-Miranda and Millie were seated together near the front of the coach. A thought occurred to Alice-Miranda and she let out a small gasp.

'What's the matter?' Millie asked.

'I forgot to ask Uncle Lawrence if he'd heard from Tyger Lombardi.' Alice-Miranda's hand flew to her mouth. 'I feel terrible.'

'He would have said something if he'd heard. She must be okay otherwise she would have called,' Millie said.

'What if she couldn't call?' Alice-Miranda realised that rather than Lawrence giving Tyger his phone number, it probably would have been more sensible had it been the other way around.

'Oh yeah,' Millie agreed. 'I wouldn't worry too much. She looks like a woman who can take care of herself. She'll be fine.'

But there was something niggling at Alice-Miranda. An uneasy feeling. She resolved to talk to her uncle as soon as he arrived later that night – maybe he could make some calls to be sure that Tyger was okay.

Chapter 34

Aislin Devine sat on her front porch, basking in the warmth of the late afternoon sun. She must have dozed off, because when she opened her eyes, she wondered if her time had finally come. She looked up at a cluster of clouds the shade of molten lava that were casting shards of light onto the desert landscape. Surely this had to be heaven, she thought, but a loud burst of foul-smelling wind from Boomer brought her plummeting back to earth. Aislin rested the book she'd been reading on her lap and watched a hawk soaring high in the distance. It was catching the updraught and circling, no doubt ready to swoop on a creature below. From her own eagle's nest over-looking the valley, she had a spectacular view of the cliffs and the canyon beyond.

Things had changed since Garber's last visit. It was as if his chatter had set her teeth on edge. She didn't need no city folk turning up out here. No siree, she and Boomer were very happy on their own. From the little she knew about the outside world, she got the impression it was a mean place. She much preferred to live among the characters of her books, knowing that it was all made up. Real life was harsh. She had come to know that at a young age. Aislin had no desire to relive the past, although her heart ached for it some days. It ached for him and what might have been if the events of that fateful day could somehow be altered. If the accident had never occurred. She squeezed her eyes shut, banishing the thoughts from her mind. Most of the time that worked, but lately not so much.

She'd started dreaming again too, waking up in a lather of sweat as if she'd fallen from a hole in the sky – or off the edge of the canyon. It was the noise that got to her. How could she dream so loudly? It just didn't seem possible.

She let the book slip to the ground and rubbed the tops of her thighs. They'd been aching ever since she and Boomer had walked along the ridge to see the camp site. Garber was right. There were fancy trailers everywhere and it looked as though they'd built some extravagant facilities too. But no one had bothered her and that was exactly the way she liked it. They'd be gone soon enough.

The dog lumbered down the few steps off the porch and began to howl.

'Stop that, you silly old goat,' Aislin scolded, shaking her head. 'You'll be waking the neighbours.'

But she knew that wasn't true. Closest thing she had to neighbours was the people of the Hualapai Indian Nation on the other side of the ridge. And they were miles away, where the tourists go to see the canyon.

'Come on then, Boomer. It's time to get dinner started,' she said.

The old dog wagged his tail and spun around, sliding through the screen door in front of her.

Chapter 35

The bus arrived at the camp site as the sun was setting in the western sky. The colours were nothing short of a technicolour dreamcoat of pinks, blues and greys against a backdrop of rocky red mountains. The landscape was now mostly devoid of the Joshua trees that were strewn across the countryside from where they'd exited the highway. They'd passed through a few tiny towns – some with boarded-up buildings and only one or two shops, and others clearly aimed at tourists, with all manner of strange souvenirs on offer. It was hard to imagine living all the way out here in the desert and Alice-Miranda had found herself wondering what people did for work. She imagined it was mostly tourism-related, although she had spotted some longhorn cattle roaming about too. For a short time, they'd travelled on the famous Route 66, which in its heyday was the main road that traversed America from coast to coast. In more recent times it had been replaced by fast, wide freeways, but it was still popular with the tourists.

'I don't think I've ever seen anything so beautiful,' Jacinta gasped, as she jumped down to the ground, with Lucas and Millie behind her.

'I have,' the boy whispered, looking at her shyly.

Caprice gagged. 'I think I just vomited in my mouth,' she groaned. She'd had to suffer through the lovebirds holding hands the whole way there. At one point they'd fallen asleep with Jacinta resting her head on Lucas's shoulder. It was all too much.

The camp site was something to behold with at least twenty enormous caravans lined up and another five or so smaller ones. The Americans referred to them as RVs – recreational vehicles – and they were nothing short of jaw-dropping. A half-dozen of the trailers had to be pulled by prime movers while others looked more like giant converted coaches. In addition to the caravans, there was a large open shelter with a fully equipped outdoor kitchen and tables for dining as well as a convoy of catering trucks. A little further away on a small ridge overlooking the site was an enormous fire pit with seating logs surrounding it. Millie thought it looked perfect for an evening singalong and could almost taste the toasted marshmallows. Over on the southern side of the camp was a portable shower and toilet block. Not your usual port-a-potties, these were glamorous with a capital 'G' and the advertising on the outside said they were six-star, whatever that meant. In the far corner of the grounds, Millie spotted some horses that had been corralled into several yards.

Parked on the perimeter were technical vans complete with satellite dishes and small overhead cranes. The whole place was crawling with crew members who were busy rolling out lengths of cable and checking equipment. Apparently, there were a bunch more staff a mile or so away over the hill where the set had been built and they would start filming tomorrow.

Emmy read out the sleeping arrangements, hoping that everyone would be reasonably happy as she didn't have too much leeway with regards to moving people around. Shooting on location was an expensive business and she was well aware that the logistics team had only just organised enough accommodation for the cast and crew. She had heard that some of the junior staff members might have to be put up in tents, but it didn't look like it had come to that yet.

Alice-Miranda was sharing with Millie and Jacinta while Sloane and Sophie were bunking with Caprice. That was probably for the best, given the recent sparks between Jacinta and their leading lady. Lucas was sharing with Sep, and Blade had a trailer all to himself.

'What about me?' Sasha asked.

Aviva Goldberg patted her son's arm. 'We're together, booboola.'

The boy's face turned redder than the desert sands. 'But how come Blade doesn't have to share with his mum?' he blurted.

Aviva pouted, her enhanced lips taking on a life of their own. 'Doesn't my baby want to be with his mamma?'

Caprice giggled, although Millie stared her down. She hated that Sasha was being humiliated and his stupid mother didn't even realise what she was doing.

'No, I don't,' Sasha replied. 'I want to be with my friends like everyone else.'

Blade felt sorry for the kid. He had everything in the world but friends and, really, he wasn't a bad guy – maybe a bit clueless, that's all. 'You can share with me,' Blade said, much to his mother's surprise.

'Really?' Sasha's eyes widened in disbelief. Blade gave a nod. 'Thanks,' Sasha said, the corners of his mouth lifting up into a smile.

Tish sidled over to her son. 'Since when are you two friends?'

Blade shrugged. 'Everyone deserves a second chance and he's actually really nice.'

Tish's stomach twisted. She wondered exactly what her son meant. He'd better not have done any secret deals with the kid behind her back or there would be trouble. She wasn't planning to give that ten thousand dollars back to whoever had left it under the doormat.

The children dashed off to explore their accommodation and get settled in, but not before Emmy told them to meet at the fire pit for a briefing at five o'clock, when they'd be given their shooting schedule and arrangements for tomorrow.

Millie leapt onto the steps of the trailer and wrenched opened the door. She almost fell out backwards. 'Whoa,' she breathed, once she'd regained her balance. 'I'm going to have to convince Mum and Dad to get a new caravan. This makes ours look like a sardine tin.'

Alice-Miranda and Jacinta scurried in behind her.

'It's huge!' Jacinta walked into the middle of the vehicle, running her hand along the plush sectional sofa and the timber dining table. In the centre of the palatial trailer was a complete kitchen with a fully stocked refrigerator and a pantry containing all manner of snacks, including Millie's latest local favourites, Twinkies and Oreo cookies. Opposite the kitchen was a lounge and dining area with a sizeable flat-screen television and reclining leather lounges.

Millie ran to the back of the vehicle and pushed open a door. 'Bags this bedroom,' she called from a twin room with its own en suite. 'You can share with me if you like, Alice-Miranda.'

'Sounds great,' the girl replied, as she hurried to see the space for herself.

'Enjoy yourselves back there. I've found my room,' Jacinta called from the other end of the beast, where she was checking out a queen bedroom that also boasted its very own bathroom.

The girls met again in the middle.

'See how the sides of the trailer pop out from the main part?' Millie said, examining the way the walls were like rectangular boxes.

'I think I could get used to Hollywood-style camping,' Alice-Miranda said with a smile.

'Glamping, did you say?' Jacinta grinned and flicked what she thought was a light switch, only to realise that one side of the van was moving inwards.

'What did you do?' Millie grimaced, hoping they weren't about to be crushed. The floor seemed to be inching towards the other side of the room.

Jacinta quickly flicked the switch the other way and the floor crept back out again. 'Sorry. Note to self – that's not a light switch.'

The children were settled in no time and soon headed out to see what everyone else's trailers were like. Sloane and Sophie gave the girls a speedy tour of their identical home away from home. Caprice had claimed the biggest room and was busy unpacking her things. Just before five o'clock, the children made their way over to the fire pit to find out what the following day would bring.

Chapter 36

Tyger Lombardi lay on the back seat of the SUV under a blanket, her mouth still covered with tape. At least he'd removed the blindfold, she thought to herself. They'd been driving for hours. At first she could see the city streetlights, but that had all disappeared hours ago. He had stopped at a place she didn't know and let her go to the toilet in an abandoned roadhouse. She'd looked around, desperate for an escape route or a phone box, disappointingly finding neither. Where would she go, anyway?

She had no idea how far they were from civilisation. Tyger had looked up at the jewel-encrusted sky and said a silent prayer, hoping that a car would pass and she could make a run for it. But that didn't happen, and before she knew it she was back in the car again. She was starving too and couldn't remember the last time she'd eaten.

Tyger had been fidgeting since being back in the car and had finally managed to get her hands out from behind her. She slowly prised the strip of duct tape from her lips, biting her tongue to stop herself from screaming. It seemed to take forever to achieve her goal. She wouldn't need her upper lip waxed for years, that was for sure. Tyger nibbled at the rope that bound her hands until at long last it fell away. She hastily untied her legs. Now she just had to get him to stop the car.

'I'm hungry,' she whined.

'Hey! What do you think you're doing back there?' He braked suddenly and the car veered off the side of the road into the gravel, pulling up hard. This was her chance. Tyger grabbed her camera bag and, before he had time to unbuckle his seatbelt, she was out of the car and running into the pitch-black night. Tyger had no idea where she was going or what was in front of her, but all those years of working with a personal trainer were about to pay off. They had to. There was no going back now.

'You think you're so clever, Tyger, but you're not. I'm coming for you,' he yelled as she scaled the hillside. A torch light flashed, seeking her out.

Tyger ran higher and higher, scrabbling over boulders and jumping behind bushes. She didn't turn around until she'd reached the top of the hill. Back down on the road, the car headlights had disappeared.

Ahead of her, far away in the distance, was a light. She watched long enough to know that it hadn't moved. Maybe it was a house. She had to get there, no matter what.

Tyger kept running and falling and grasping at rocks until the light shone brighter. Every now and then she stopped and listened, but there was nothing except the hooting of an owl and an occasional skirmish in the undergrowth. She didn't even want to think about what was making those noises. Who knew if there were coyotes or other wild animals out here.

Tyger was close enough now to see that her

hunch was right. There was a house. She was going to be okay. The thought crossed her mind that whoever lived there might not be very pleased to see her. After all, it did seem a long way from anywhere, but maybe she was wrong. Maybe it was just the edge of a town. Tyger felt as if her legs were made of lead. She could barely put one foot in front of the other, but this was no time to give up. And then she missed her footing and stumbled on a rock.

'Ow!' she yelled. The pain in her ankle was searing.

There was a wire fence around the boundary and she heard the guttural growls of a big dog. Big and hopefully docile. Now was not the time to be eaten by a vicious hound. She'd come too far for that.

Tyger heard a squeaky door.

'Boomer, what's out there?' a woman called.

'Please help me!' Tyger whimpered. She had almost reached the fence when the huge beast raced towards her and knocked her flat. Tyger raised her hands to protect her throat to protect herself, waiting for the creature's jaws to take hold when she realised that she was being licked.

'Boomer, what have you found?' the woman asked.

'Hello,' Tyger cried, with more volume this time. 'Help!'

'Good heavens!' The woman grabbed a torch and shuffled down off the porch and into the yard. She shone the light onto Tyger, who was bleeding from deep scratches on her arms and face. 'Boomer, get off her!' she demanded. The dog did as he was bid. The woman looked at Tyger's face. 'Oh my, whatever's happened to you?'

Tyger rolled over and pushed herself up, unable to bear weight on her left leg.

'Come with me,' the woman urged. She took Tyger's arm and guided her to the porch. Tyger hobbled up the few steps and through the front door with the dog close behind. Once inside, the elderly woman helped Tyger into a recliner covered with crocheted throws. 'Heavens be, where on earth did you come from?'

Tyger's lip began to tremble and she promptly burst into tears.

Chapter 37

'Good morning, Uncle Lawrence,' Alice-Miranda greeted the man. He was seated on a bench in the outdoor dining area, tucking into a huge plate of eggs and bacon. She slipped in beside him with her own plate of pancakes and maple syrup. There were three chefs on hand catering for the early risers.

'Hello sweetheart,' Lawrence said between bites. He gestured to his plate. 'Please don't dob me into Charlotte for this. She's worried about my arteries.'

Alice-Miranda smiled at him. 'Your secret's safe with me. What time did you arrive last night?'

'It was after midnight,' Lawrence said, stifling a yawn. 'I wasn't sure if we'd even make it.'

Alice-Miranda frowned at him. 'Was there a problem?'

'That's not the half of it,' Lawrence sighed. 'Frau Furtwangler will be here this evening. Apparently, someone erased Caprice and Sasha's solo tracks, so she's bringing a portable studio out to record them again. They won't know that yet, so probably best not to mention it. Then there were problems with the equipment and we had to wait half the day for a technician to sort it out. It was the strangest thing. Someone had cut several cables, but everyone in the place denied responsibility.' Lawrence ate another mouthful of his breakfast.

'That does sound odd,' Alice-Miranda said. She had begun to wonder if there was a saboteur in their midst – it was far more likely than a curse. 'I wanted to ask whether you had heard from Tyger Lombardi. I've been thinking about her a lot.'

Lawrence pulled his phone from his pocket and showed it to her. 'She sent me a text yesterday morning to say that she was fine and there was nothing to worry about. She said she got her camera back and she was going to leave town for a while.'

'Well, that's a relief,' Alice-Miranda said.

Lawrence mopped up the last of his runny eggs with a piece of toast and stood up. 'Sorry to have to run, darling, but I'm expected in wardrobe and I think you need to be in hair and make-up soon too.'

'Yes, we do.' She nodded as Millie and Jacinta walked over to the table and sat down.

'See you at the bus, girls.' Lawrence gave a wave and disappeared into the makeshift village.

'Uncle Lawrence said that Tyger Lombardi is fine. She got her camera back and now she's taking a holiday,' Alice-Miranda told the girls.

'That's one less thing to worry about,' Millie said, as Caprice stormed towards them. From the look on the girl's face, someone was about to cop it. 'Especially now that trouble is headed our way.'

'What's the matter with you?' Jacinta asked Caprice.

'My boots are missing! Someone has stolen them,' the girl huffed, glaring at her.

Everyone looked down and noticed that she was indeed wearing ballet flats instead of her beautiful brown boots.

'Have you checked with Mrs Sparrow?' Alice-Miranda asked.

'Of course I have and she says that I must have lost them because she personally put them into my trailer last night,' Caprice said.

'Is there a spare pair somewhere?' Millie asked.

'I have to wear *those* boots because they're the ones I've worn the whole time and they are antiques and so there are none like them anywhere!' Caprice fumed. 'If I can't find them, we're going to have to reshoot everything from last week!'

'As if we'd have to do that just because your boots are different,' Millie scoffed.

Caprice rolled her eyes. 'You clearly know nothing about movies. This film *is* cursed.'

'We'll help you look for them,' Alice-Miranda offered. 'Perhaps Mrs Sparrow put them in our trailer and she thought that was where you were sleeping. They are identical.'

'I'm not going,' Millie said. 'I need to eat breakfast and then we've got to be in hair and make-up in fifteen minutes.'

'Whatever!' Caprice turned on her heel and stormed in the direction of the girls' trailer with Alice-Miranda scurrying after her.

Chapter 38

'Where have you two been?' Emmy was standing beside the bus door, tapping on her clipboard. Everyone was on board and waiting for Caprice and Alice-Miranda, who had raced from the hair and make-up trailer, having finally located Caprice's lost boots under Jacinta's bed.

'Ask *her* why we're late!' Caprice stomped up the steps and pointed at Jacinta, who was sitting beside Sophie in the front seat.

Jacinta had no idea what the girl was talking

about, but Caprice made sure that everyone else on the bus was fully acquainted with her theory that Jacinta had hidden her boots because she was jealous of Caprice and wanted the movie to fail.

Harold Lipp exhaled loudly. 'Sit down, young lady, and don't be so utterly ridiculous. We have no time for this sort of nonsense. There is a film to be made and if you can't get along with your castmates then I suggest we all pack up and go home right now,' he ordered.

Caprice thudded down onto the very back seat, shocked that Mr Lipp of all people would speak to her like that. Unfortunately for the girl, no one believed a word of her nonsense either.

With Mrs Goldberg and Mrs Crawford off to do some sightseeing, Mr Lipp and Emmy were accompanying the children to the set. The vehicle bumped over the track as they took in the breathtaking scenery around them. Although she was doing her best to maintain her sulk, there was only so long that Caprice could focus on the floor with all the distracting 'oohs and aahs' of her fellow passengers. She glanced out the window and was immediately mesmerised by the surroundings. The landscape of monolithic ranges rising up from the red dirt were spectacular. Along the edge of the roadway, which Alice-Miranda had wondered might have been made especially for the movie, was a mismatched landscape of scrubby bushes, some tall and thorny, others squat and barely rooted to the ground. In the distance the canyon with its plateaus and cliffs was like nothing they'd ever seen before.

'Are there rattlesnakes out here?' Lucas asked loudly, suddenly thinking that this country did look a bit dangerous.

'Yes, siree,' the driver said. 'And scorpions and coyotes and mountain lions and condors among other things.'

'Then I'm not getting off the bus,' Caprice stated.

'Well, it's going to be tricky to film your scenes from in here,' Blade said. 'It's okay. I'm sure we won't see any of those things and, if we do, they'd be more scared of us than we are of them.'

'Don't you be so sure of that, young man,' the driver said. But he was interrupted by Emmy, who thought now might be a good time to go over the call sheet for the day and make sure that everyone knew what they were doing. She didn't want to think about all those creatures either.

'So today we have a couple of challenging scenes

and I know that some of you have opted to do your own riding while others will be using stunt doubles. I can assure you there's nothing too difficult and the horses are beautifully trained and will do whatever you tell them. But if you've changed your mind and would rather not ride, let me know and we'll work something out.' Emmy was hoping that wasn't the case as, contrary to what she'd originally been told, there were only so many of the stunt crew who could pass for children.

'Look at the canyon!' Millie exclaimed, pointing out the bus as the full scope and scale of the natural wonder came into view.

'Hey, there's the sound stage,' Sep said, as the children caught sight of the tiny town that had been constructed on the red plain. There were trucks and equipment everywhere, and parked a little further away on a flat piece of ground were two helicopters that had just landed.

'Movies are mad.' The boy shook his head, still pinching himself that he was actually part of the whole thing.

Chapter 39

Tyger Lombardi's eyes sprang open and she flinched with fear. For a second she had no memory of where she was until a long tongue appeared over the edge of the bed and licked her on the chin.

'Yuck,' she groaned, pushing the bloodhound away.

'Boomer, you leave that poor girl alone,' a voice called from somewhere outside the room.

Tyger shuffled up on the pillows and scratched Boomer's head. He yawned and she quickly covered her nose. 'Urgh, that's some morning breath you've got there, boy.'

Boomer wagged his tail on high speed as if to agree.

Tyger heard the rattle of china before the old woman appeared with a tea tray, on which sat a cup and saucer and two pieces of toast with butter.

'How are you feeling this morning?' the woman asked. She balanced the tray as she cleared a space on a round table that was piled high with books in the corner of the room.

'Better, I think, thank you,' Tyger said, despite the fact her ankle was throbbing. 'Who are you and where am I?'

'I'm Aislin and this is Boomer and you're in the Arizona desert,' the woman replied. 'Can't really tell you the address because we don't have one.'

'You told me that last night, didn't you?' Tyger began to remember. Aislin passed her the teacup and placed the plate of toast on the other side of the bed, away from Boomer's reach.

'I need to call the police,' Tyger said.

The old woman moved a pile of books from a chair and placed them on the floor, then sat down. 'I'm afraid I don't have a telephone,' she said.

Tyger looked at her in disbelief. 'What do you mean?'

'I don't have a telephone,' Aislin repeated.

'But you live in the middle of nowhere.' Tyger's heart thumped hard and she began to feel dizzy. Her whole lower leg was hot and painful.

'It's not quite the middle of nowhere, but it's close, I grant you that,' Aislin said with a nod.

'But you have a car?' Tyger asked.

Aislin shook her head. 'Not for the past twenty years, I haven't.'

'How do you go anywhere?' Tyger asked.

'Well, we don't these days. Do we, Boomer? We're happy here on our own. Garber will be back in a month with our supplies.'

'What if you get sick or there's an emergency?' Tyger was finding it hard to believe what she was hearing.

'Things seem to take care of themselves,' Aislin said with a kind smile. 'And, honey, I'm too old to care about getting sick. If it's time to go, I'm ready.'

'What about neighbours?' Tyger asked. There had to be someone within walking distance who had a means of communicating with the outside world.

'There's the Hualapai Nation, the Indian reserve about twenty miles to the west. The last time I spotted someone would be two years ago. There's the odd trekker, but mostly it's just us and that's the way we like it.'

Tyger felt a growing discomfort. The woman was a hermit and she'd barged into her life out of nowhere. 'I'm sorry for coming here,' she apologised. 'I'll be going as soon as I can.'

Aislin smiled at her. 'No, don't you be sorry about that. You needed my help.' It had surprised the old woman how much she didn't mind the company. 'You won't be walking anywhere for a while. Your ankle's a mess. I bandaged it last night, though I think it's going to take some time for the swelling to go down and you're gonna have one heck of a bruise.'

Tyger studied the old woman's face. Her violet eyes were mesmerising and, despite the ravages of time and age and something much worse, she had a classic beauty that must once have been quite breathtaking. Among the wrinkles, scars like tiny railway tracks crisscrossed her chin and cheeks and forehead. She must have been in an accident, although now didn't seem the right time to ask.

'So, there's no one close by at all.' Tyger gulped. It was beginning to dawn on her that she might be stuck out here for days, weeks even. What if he was still looking for her? What if, in the daylight, he discovered where she was? He hadn't ever said what he was planning to do with her, but she suspected that if he'd brought her all the way out here to the desert, it wasn't to throw her a party.

Tyger nibbled at her toast even though she didn't feel much like eating. She was sore all over from the running and tripping on heaven knows what. Her arms were scratched and, apart from the throbbing pain in her ankle, she could feel something under the skin in her left palm. She touched it and winced in pain.

'Would you like me to take a look at that?' Aislin asked, noticing the woman's discomfort.

Tyger wondered if Aislin could see anything but she quickly disappeared and returned with a small first-aid kit and a magnifying glass. She set to and soon found the culprit. Tyger flinched as Aislin squeezed a spike about half an inch long from the heel of her palm.

'Oh, that's a nasty one. Glad we found it or it could've been infected in a day or two,' Aislin said.

She placed the offending prickle into a small silver kidney dish. 'I haven't had one of those in quite a while, but the last time – oh my, it was a beast of a thing. Took me a whole day of digging to be rid of it.'

Tyger thanked her as she swabbed the wound with antiseptic and covered it with a plaster. Suddenly, she remembered her camera. 'Did I have a bag with me last night?' Tyger asked. She knew she'd taken it out of the car, but whether or not it made it all the way to the house with her, she couldn't recall.

Aislin tottered out of the room and reappeared a minute later, placing the bag on the bed.

'Oh, that's something I guess,' Tyger said. She unzipped the case and pulled out her camera. It was still in one piece, thankfully. She dug around and checked the lenses – there were three in separate compartments and they were all intact. Then she unzipped another compartment on the side. 'So that's where I put it,' she said to herself, relieved to have found the Finkelstein's bag she'd been searching for over the past couple of weeks. At least she had something to read while her ankle healed. Looking around at the piles of books, actually, it seemed she'd have plenty to keep her occupied.

'I think you should try to get some rest,' Aislin said.

Tyger yawned. She had no idea of the time, but she was drowsy and the offer to sleep was tempting. Although she needed to work out how she was going to get out of here too.

'Do you think he'll come for me?' Tyger whispered, suddenly aware that being here had put Aislin's life in danger too.

'If he gets anywhere near this place, I have a few deterrents, along with old Boomer here, who's been known to scare off everything from coyotes to mountain lions,' the old woman said.

'Maybe I'll just close my eyes for a little while then,' Tyger said. She felt overwhelmed with exhaustion, as though the struggle last night had sucked every ounce of energy from her body. Tyger lay back down and Aislin cleared away the plate and cup and saucer. She then lifted the bag from the bed and sat it on the floor.

'Rest up. And give me a yell if you need anything,' the old woman said, as she walked to the door. 'Come on, Boomer, you can help me collect the eggs.'

But Tyger didn't hear a thing. She was already fast asleep.

Chapter 40

When the children hopped off the four-wheel-drive bus, Alice-Miranda immediately noticed Andreas King. He was dashing all over the place like a flea in a bottle, checking this and that, but mostly scratching his head with a look of complete and utter confusion.

'Aren't the horses beautiful?' Millie said, pointing at the twenty beasts saddled western-style and ready for action. They were tied up to a long hitching rail over by the saloon.

'You won't get me on one,' Sloane murmured to Sophie.

'Me either,' Sasha said quietly.

Millie and Jacinta scampered over to take a closer look while Emmy darted off to find out how long it would be until they started shooting.

As Alice-Miranda wandered among the crew, marvelling at the extraordinary set-up with cameras on miniature railway lines, and giant overhead booms attached to small tractor-like machines, she caught sight of a figure out of the corner of her eye. She gasped and backtracked, hiding behind a piece of equipment. It was them! The two men from the studio lot who'd been talking about Tyger Lombardi.

This time the man she'd spoken to out the front of the theatre wasn't dressed in black. He was in casual clothes, as if he was just one of the workmen. The shorter, rounder-looking fellow seemed to be part of the crew too. The pair was deep in conversation.

'So, I hear Costa Rica is nice this time of year,' the pudgy fellow said with a grin.

'I'm sure it is,' the taller man replied, deadpan. 'You'll have to help me find her, though, if you fancy a trip.'

Alice-Miranda wondered what he was talking about. Tyger Lombardi had told Uncle Lawrence that she had got her camera back. But how, if she didn't get it from him? The child thought back to their last encounter with Tyger. Hadn't Millie mentioned that the fellows had been heading to bungalow three? Alice-Miranda smiled, thinking that Tyger had probably been clever enough to go and find the camera herself. Good for her. But didn't that mean she might still be in danger? Alice-Miranda would ask her uncle later on and see if Bob Loy had said anything to him about Tyger and the black bag. After all, he was meant to drive her back to the studio entrance.

Alice-Miranda peered around to see if the men were still there, but they'd moved on. She spotted Andreas King and hurried over to him. 'Hello Mr King.'

'What is it now?' he snapped, not even turning around.

'Sorry,' the child said. 'I thought you might appreciate some help, or maybe a friendly face.'

He spun around, his brow creased in exasperation. 'Oh, Alice-Miranda, it's you. I'm sorry. It just feels like nothing is going right out here today.'

Her forehead puckered. 'What do you mean?'

'Well, for starters, the generator has conked out and a whole lot of the batteries are flat – we need the power to get them charged so we can use the cameras. Several of the crew have come down with what appears to be food poisoning and I've misplaced my script file, which has all my notes in it,' the man said, finally pausing to take a breath.

Alice-Miranda bit her lip. This shoot did seem to be plagued with odd setbacks, for which there had to be a rational explanation. 'That does sound like an awful lot of problems. Do you think we'll be able to shoot today?' she asked.

'We have to. I've only got you guys for a few more days. If we don't get it done, this movie is going to be a total bust,' Andreas said, running a hand through his hair. 'So much for my big break, hey? Mr Goldberg was crazy to ask me to do this and I was mad to say yes. The guy's a fool and I'm an even bigger one.'

Alice-Miranda smiled at him. 'You're doing a great job. It's not your fault all those things have happened. Do you remember when you last had your file?'

'It was in my hands a half-hour ago. I put it down and, when I went back to get it, it was gone,' the man said, shaking his head.

'Leave it to me,' Alice-Miranda said confidently. 'I'll fetch the others and we'll go over this place with a fine-tooth comb.'

Before Andreas had time to object, the tiny child was off. She raced back to her castmates and gathered them together, explaining the situation.

'So, let's find Andreas's script then,' Jacinta said.

'And I'll take a look at the generator,' Blade offered.

'Since when did you know anything about machinery?' Caprice scoffed at the lad. 'Aren't you a Hollywood boy?'

'Actually, I'm a farm boy from Idaho. My dad has taught me heaps of stuff,' Blade said.

'That's cool.' Sasha nodded. 'I wish I knew how things worked.'

'I might be able to help too,' Sophie weighed in.

The children looked at her quizzically.

'I like pulling things apart and putting them back together,' the girl said with a shrug. 'My dad had an old motorbike, which I took to bits and reassembled and I got it running again.'

The group split up with most of them going to look for Andreas's script file and the other three headed to see if they could help with the generator.

Sasha wasn't going to be any use, but he was happy to provide moral support.

The children hunted high and low for the script – under chairs, on top of cameras, in the big black metal boxes that were used to carry the equipment. After almost half an hour of frantic searching, it was Jacinta who came up trumps.

'Found it!' she shouted, and ran back towards the crew. Her friends came running from all around the set. Camera and boom operators, technicians, the best boy and various other staff were bewildered by the child who was yelling about and turning cartwheels.

'Where was it?' Millie panted.

'It was the oddest thing,' the girl said, as she held on to the prize. 'It was in the back of the horse truck over there, underneath the straw. I almost missed it, but I kicked at the straw, thinking I was being completely ridiculous, when I connected with it.'

Alice-Miranda thought it was very strange indeed. 'Someone must have put it there because Andreas said he'd set it down on his director's chair and then it was gone. Come on, let's get it back to him.'

The children hurried over to the man, whose face was red, having moments ago had an argument with the director of photography about the way they were going to shoot the first scene – if they got to shoot at all.

'Excuse me, Mr King,' Alice-Miranda said. 'Jacinta found your folder.'

He looked at the girls, his bottom lip trembling.

'It was in the horse truck,' the child added.

At that point, the director burst into tears. 'Thank you,' he sobbed, wiping at his eyes. 'This movie's cursed. I should have realised when I took it on. There's a reason it never made it to the screen the first time.'

'What are you talking about?' Alice-Miranda asked, offering the man a tissue. She and Millie had seen the photographs in the Goldbergs' attic and had assumed that the film had been finished and screened.

'Oh, never mind. I'm just exhausted,' Andreas sniffled. He blew his nose. 'Thank you. If only they could get the generator going again we might be able to start.'

The diesel engine clattered to life, shattering the desert peace. There was a cheer over by the truck and some hearty thanks to Blade, who had worked out what the problem was.

'Is that what I think it is?' Andreas looked as if he was about to burst into tears again.

The girls nodded.

'Let's get this show back on the road!' The man started dancing, pulling some very cool moves.

The children laughed, and someone blasted a song over the speakers. Soon everyone was dancing. They say happiness is contagious and it was none more apparent than in that moment, when it seemed as though the entire cast and crew were up for some fun. Even a couple of the horses looked like they were busting a few moves. Emmy raced around and gathered everyone into their positions so that, finally, they were ready to begin.

Chapter 41

The sun was setting over the mountains when Andreas called a wrap on filming. For the first time since they'd started working on the project, everything had run like clockwork and they were ahead of schedule going into day two. The man couldn't have been happier, although he was completely spent.

'You guys were amazing.' He beamed at the children, who had tackled their horse riding and various other scenes faultlessly. Considering they'd had the helicopters buzzing overhead with cameraman filming from on high as well as on the ground, the beasts had behaved impeccably. Apparently, they were quite used to it. Andreas had filmed any scenes involving Blade and Sasha's characters twice so that he had Blade in the lead and Sasha as support and vice versa. There was a change of costume required each time, but Mrs Sparrow had done a brilliant job making sure the clothes were identical and the boys soon had their transformations down to a fine art. The kids and Andreas had decided this was the best way to do it. That way, none of the adults need know what was going on until the movie was in the can and the director could choose which worked better. Andreas's legs had gone to jelly when he had Blade in the lead; he was utterly terrified that the parents were going to turn up on set, having escaped from their sightseeing tour, but Emmy had done well, keeping them busy the whole day.

Come half past five, the group was back at camp and enjoying hot showers before dinner.

'Today was fun, wasn't it?' Millie said, as she hung up her costume in the wardrobe in their room.

'Patch is the loveliest pony,' Alice-Miranda said. 'And he's so cute with those big brown splodges all over his coat. I just wish Bonaparte's manners were half as good as his. Perhaps I should ask if Miss Connie makes international house calls for badly behaved beasts,' Alice-Miranda said, referring to the woman who oversaw the horses. Miss Connie was impressive – fit and wiry and as strong as an ox. In her jeans and checked shirt, cowboy hat and boots, the woman looked as if she'd walked straight off a ranch – which was quite likely. 'Emmy said she's the best horse whisperer in the whole country.'

'Chops could probably do with some equine etiquette too. I think he's picked up a few bad habits from his best buddy. Did you know he pulled a great chunk of my hair out a couple of weeks ago? I wonder who he learned that from.' Millie stuffed her feet into her sandshoes and laced them up, then grabbed a jacket. 'Come on,' she said. 'I'm starving.'

Alice-Miranda gave Jacinta a shout to see if she was ready too. She quickly joined them and the girls headed outside. The desert air was chilly and someone had lit the fire pit. Several of the children and adults were already seated around it.

Aviva Goldberg was holding court with Tish Crawford and some of the crew, already reminiscing about the amazing day they'd had over at the West Rim of the canyon, which catered for tourists. The rhinestones on Aviva Goldberg's high-heeled cowboy boots glinted in the firelight.

'I think your mother might have some competition in the shoe stakes,' Millie whispered to Sloane, who snickered appreciatively.

'Oh, please don't remind me. Thank goodness Mummy didn't come on this trip or she'd have been dazzling everyone with her footwear too.' The children giggled. Sloane was referring to September Sykes's penchant for sparkly wedge-heeled trainers, which the woman had worn and lost and, sadly, at least in her daughter's opinion, managed to replace during their trip to China.

'Yoohoo! Kids, come and join us,' Aviva called, spotting the children gathering at the buffet. The chefs had produced an impressive display of nibbles and snacks before dinner.

'You've got to hear about our day,' Tish added. 'And it's not over yet, because we're going to Las Vegas for the night!'

'Booboola,' Avivia cried. 'Bring mamma a bowl of those corn chips and that delicious salsa dip. You know I hate flying on an empty stomach.'

Sasha's face lit up like the campfire. 'Why does she have to do that?' he murmured to Millie.

'It's okay,' she said, touching the boy's elbow. 'No one's paying any attention.'

'No, of course we're not, booboola.' Blade leaned over the lad's shoulder and grinned. 'I'm kidding. Your mother isn't half as bad as mine. One minute she wants me to be a star and the next minute she's telling me to back off. I don't get her at all.'

Sasha rolled his eyes. 'I think they're probably both a bit crazy.'

Blade walked up to the fire pit while Millie helped Sasha procure Mrs Goldberg's request. In the distance, the whir of helicopter rotors began to hum.

'Have you seen Uncle Lawrence?' Alice-Miranda asked Emmy, who had just poured herself a glass of mineral water.

'He and Alexa have gone in one of the helicopters to Phoenix for a fundraiser they were both committed to ages ago. They'll be back in the morning. The poor man never stops,' Emmy replied.

'I think we could say the same about you,' Alice-Miranda said, and smiled at the woman.

'Some days it kind of feels like that,' Emmy admitted. 'But it's a great job, so I really can't complain.' She gulped her drink and placed the empty glass down on a tray. 'Sounds as though the other helicopter's ready to leave. Excuse me, sweetheart, I need to round up the travellers.'

Emmy hurried off to organise Mrs Goldberg and Mrs Crawford. She felt immensely pleased with herself for thinking they'd enjoy a night in Vegas and, fortunately, the women had leapt at the idea. Emmy was aware of Andreas's plans for the kids and she really didn't want to be anywhere near Aviva Goldberg when she found out what was going on.

Quite a few members of the crew were heading over to get something to eat and drink. Alice-Miranda was in the middle of pouring herself a mineral water when she turned and let out a tiny gasp. The two men from the bungalow were right behind her. She'd noticed the pudgy one on the set a couple of times during the day and she thought she'd seen the other fellow getting into one of the helicopters, but until now she hadn't seen them up close. She'd told Millie about her earlier encounter, though she was yet to catch up with her uncle and ask him if perhaps he should talk to someone about them – probably Eli Goldberg – when he could.

The taller fellow looked right at her, seemingly lost in thought, then snapped out of it and poured himself a cola. It was as if she was invisible, which was a relief.

'So, what did you see up there?' the shorter chap asked.

'There's a house over the top of the ridge, if you could call it a house. More like a couple of trailers, but there's a garden and it looks as though it's inhabited,' he said. 'Its beyond me why anyone would want to live out here. Can you imagine it?'

Alice-Miranda knew that she shouldn't have been listening, but she couldn't help herself. She moved along the buffet and stalled at the buffalo wings, piling her plate as she waited for them to catch up to her.

'I'm going up there tonight,' the taller man said. 'There's a road. I saw it snaking from the valley.'

'Do you think you'll find her?' the shorter fellow asked.

His friend looked at Alice-Miranda's plate, on which she'd absently placed more than a dozen wings. 'You hungry, kiddo?'

'Oh, they're for my friends,' she said quietly, not wanting to say too much in case he remembered her voice.

His eyes narrowed. 'Have we met before?'

'I don't think so,' Alice-Miranda said, and hurried along. She wanted to get out of there, but she had a very bad feeling about these two and what they were talking about. She lingered by the potato gems, adding them slowly to her plate one at a time.

'She's there, all right. From my calculations, she went up the ridge and that's the only place she'd have come across. And if she's not then I'd say she's fallen into a very big hole.'

'Why wouldn't she have called someone?' the pudgy fellow asked.

The taller man pulled a mobile phone from his pocket.

'Oh, nice,' the shorter man said with a grin. 'But surely whoever lives there has a landline.'

The taller bloke shrugged. 'We've just gotta get up there and sort her out, or else you can forget about that trip to Rio.'

Alice-Miranda grabbed another plate and added cheese and biscuits to her haul. She thought they were going to Costa Rica.

'We'll wait until everyone's gone to bed. Then we'll go hunting for our tiger and this time she won't be getting away.'

Alice-Miranda gasped.

The short fellow chuckled. 'You know I heard about dozen people a year fall off the edge of the Grand Canyon.'

'I think this year it might be lucky thirteen.' The taller man raised his eyebrows. He stared at Alice-Miranda, then it dawned on him where he'd seen her before. She was there that day, outside Grauman's Chinese Theatre. She knew something. He was sure of it.

Alice-Miranda turned and hurried over to the fire pit, where the other children swooped on her like seagulls. She disappeared among the throng, her mind racing.

Chapter 42

'I need to talk to you,' Alice-Miranda whispered to Millie. 'It's about Tyger Lombardi. She's in terrible danger.' She steered her friend to a seat away from the rest of the children.

Millie frowned. 'I thought she'd left town for a while.'

She listened intently while Alice-Miranda explained exactly what she'd heard.

'We've got to tell someone,' Millie said, standing up. 'What about Lawrence?'

Alice-Miranda shook her head. 'He and Alexa were on the first helicopter that left straight after we returned from shooting.'

'And Mrs Goldberg and Mrs Crawford have gone to Vegas.' Millie looked around the camp site. Andreas King was nowhere to be seen and Emmy had disappeared too. No one had sighted Mr Lipp for a while either, not since Frau Furtwangler had arrived to say she had a surprise for him in her trailer.

'We've got to find Tyger before they do,' Alice-Miranda said. She bit her lip and scanned the camp grounds, but the men had vanished, along with just about every other adult.

'You don't really think they'd . . .?' Millie gulped.

Alice-Miranda's mouth formed a grim line and her brows knitted together. 'They sounded serious to me.'

'We don't even know where the house is,' Millie said.

Alice-Miranda pointed to the east. 'He said it was over the ridge in that direction.'

'Let's go and find Emmy. She'll know what to do,' Millie said.

They walked back past their friends, who were chatting and enjoying their snacks.

'Are you going down to have dinner?' Jacinta asked the girls.

'Alice-Miranda's not feeling well,' Millie said. 'We're heading back to the trailer and will probably have an early night.'

Alice-Miranda shot Millie a puzzled look.

'What did you want me to tell her?' Millie said, once they'd set off. 'You know she'd want to come and maybe it's best to keep things on the down low at the moment.'

'Okay,' Alice-Miranda murmured.

As the girls wandered among the trailers, they were surprised by how deserted the camp was.

'Where do you think everyone is?' Millie asked.

Alice-Miranda shrugged. 'Maybe they have a production meeting or they're getting ready for dinner?'

In the distance the girls could hear the horses, which had been trucked back from the set. They turned a corner, when Alice-Miranda grabbed Millie's arm and pulled her behind a bank of solar panels.

'It's them!' she whispered.

The two men were closing the door to the girls' trailer.

'What were they doing in there?' Millie gasped. She stepped backwards onto a twig, which snapped underfoot.

The men looked towards the girls, who ducked out of sight, but it was too late. The taller man had spotted them. Alice-Miranda grabbed Millie's hand and the girls shot off, weaving in and out of the trailers.

'The horses,' Millie said, pointing up ahead.

Alice-Miranda could see Patch and Tonto, the horses they'd ridden that day. They were in a specially built round yard along with half a dozen others. There were two other enclosures nearby. The back of the livery truck was open and Millie charged inside. They could hear footsteps running in their direction.

'Lucky Miss Connie's organised,' Millie said, as she spied Patch and Tonto's names on the walls above their bridles. She snatched them up while Alice-Miranda opened the gate. Millie threw the girl a bridle, which she had on the pony in no time flat and Millie did the same for Tonto. The girls mounted the beasts in seconds.

They made sure to close the gate just as the men sped around the corner.

'Hey! What do you think you're doing?' the taller man yelled.

He charged at Alice-Miranda, his arms flailing as he did his best to unseat her from Patch's bare back, but he wasn't counting on the children being such experienced horseriders.

'Look out, Millie!' Alice-Miranda called, as the fellow spun around and tried to block her path. But Tonto was trained in the art of tricks and sidestepped the fellow like a seasoned football player.

The other horses in the corral began to bray and stamp their feet.

'Yah!' Alice-Miranda cried, and she and Millie wheeled around and cantered away from the camp and towards the ridge.

'Idiot!' the taller man shouted. 'We've got to get up to that house before they do or we're done for.'

Alice-Miranda and Millie cantered onwards and upwards over the rocky ground, trusting the fleet-footed ponies beneath them. It was a starry night and a half moon hung in the sky, lighting their path. As the girls climbed higher and higher, they slowed and looked back at the camp.

'What do you think they were planning to do?' Millie panted, as the ponies picked their way over the rocks and stones.

'He must have realised where he'd seen me

before, with Tyger,' the child said. 'I don't even want to think about what he was intending.'

Back down at the camp, the girls saw headlights and a car speeding off into the night. The men were after them. They had to hope and pray that this house wasn't too far away.

As the girls reached the crest of the mountain, they looked out over the vast landscape. The eerie shadows and outlines were breathtaking and terrifying at the same time. But they couldn't see a light anywhere. There was nothing but black. They were just about to turn around when, off in the distance, they spotted a dull glow. It could have been anything, but right now it was hope.

'There!' Alice-Miranda said, pointing to it. 'There's a light!'

Alice-Miranda squeezed Patch's flanks with her legs and the pony began to jog. They found a path along the top of the ridge and followed it as far as they could, then began to descend into the valley. The light was getting brighter.

But now they could hear something else too — the roar of an engine.

'Come on, Millie, we need to get there before

they do,' Alice-Miranda said, and urged Patch into a trot.

Alice-Miranda's heart was pounding as they reached the bottom of the valley and saw the light high on the hill ahead of them. Her mother would be furious, riding without a helmet, in the dark, somewhere in the Arizona desert, but they had to get to Tyger Lombardi. The woman's life depended on it.

Chapter 43

After dinner, the rest of the children had headed back to the fire pit. Sloane and Blade were taking turns toasting marshmallows on a long barbecue fork. Whoever was in charge of the site had thought of pretty much everything, with cashmere throw rugs to snuggle under and cushions for the campers to sit on. It was surprisingly cold in the desert at night. Caprice had inched herself closer and closer to Lucas. When she touched his hand under his blanket, the boy had shot into the air, as if he'd been jolted by a cattle prod. He promptly relocated next to Sep, on the other side of the fire, where they were now deep in conversation. Fortunately, Jacinta had just returned with some more marshmallows and hadn't witnessed the girl's antics.

'Has anyone seen Millie?' Sasha asked.

'She and Alice-Miranda went back to the trailer,' Jacinta said. 'Alice-Miranda wasn't feeling well.'

'Oh, okay.' Sasha frowned and sat down on one of the logs next to Blade.

'You like her, don't you?' Blade said, and although Sasha's ears blushed pink, he didn't deny it. 'She's fun.'

'I think she's really brave,' Sasha said quietly. 'I've never seen anyone as fearless on a horse, except maybe Alice-Miranda. She put me to shame.'

Blade grinned at the lad. 'You're right about that. I felt like a complete wuss today and I've grown up on a farm.'

'Oh, puh-lease.' Caprice rolled her eyes. 'Did you see me out there?'

'You were pretty good,' Blade conceded. 'And you'd be even better if you shut up about it and acted half as nicely as those other girls.'

Sophie's eyes darted up from the book she was

reading and caught Sloane's eye. The two girl's braced themselves for the onslaught.

Caprice's jaw flapped open. 'I *am* nice.'

Blade shook his head. 'I wish you were, Caprice, because then there'd be a proper reason why every time I see you my heart beats out of my chest and I feel numb when you speak to me, but perhaps that's only because you're gorgeous on the outside. If you were as lovely on the inside, I think I'd probably ask you to marry me one day, but, well, that's not going to happen anytime soon, is it?'

The other kids looked at each other, wondering what had just happened.

'Sorry?' Caprice, it seemed, was rendered speechless. 'I don't . . .'

'He was paying you a compliment, Caprice,' Sloane interjected. 'Sort of.'

Blade turned towards Sasha. 'Do you want to play cards?'

'Yeah, that would be great,' Sasha replied. 'But I have to warn you, I'm a pretty fine poker player.'

The other kids laughed.

'No, it's true – my dad taught me,' Sasha said. 'I once beat him six times straight but we only play for bottle tops.'

Lucas stood up. 'Sounds fun. Is everyone in?'

There were smiles and nods all round, except for Caprice, who was still trying to work out exactly what Blade had meant.

As the girls neared the house they heard the deep-throated barks of a big dog. The ponies trotted onto the property, lathered with sweat. Millie and Alice-Miranda leapt off and pulled the reins over the beasts' heads, hitching them to a rail on the porch.

'What is it, Boomer?' they heard a woman call.

Alice-Miranda ran up the front steps with Millie right behind her. She hammered on the door just as it swung open. An old woman dressed like Miss Connie, but with grey hair pulled back into a low bun, stood in the frame. Alice-Miranda thought she had a lovely face despite the obvious scars. The woman lowered the shotgun she was holding.

'Hello,' Alice-Miranda breathed, her voice barely audible as she gulped air into her lungs.

The dog rushed out, growling and barking.

'Boomer, you stop that and get back in here,' the woman ordered, and the hound did as he was told.

She stepped back inside and put the gun behind the door.

'Where on earth did you come from, child?' The woman looked over Alice-Miranda's shoulder and spotted Millie. 'Oh, there's two of you. I'll fetch some water.'

Alice-Miranda and Millie walked into the front room of the tiny house and were relieved to find Tyger Lombardi sitting before them.

'Alice-Miranda! What are you doing here?' Tyger pushed herself up from the settee in the crowded sitting room. She had just taken the shopping bag containing her new book out of her camera case. It fell from her hands.

'They're coming for you. We have to go. We've got to get back to the camp,' the child blurted, as the old woman handed her and Millie a glass each of water. 'I overheard them talking and I knew it was about you. The big guy from the theatre – I saw him go up in a helicopter with the crew while we were shooting today – he must have been searching for where you might be hiding. I gathered you'd escaped from him last night and, when I heard what they were planning, well, I knew we had to do something.'

Tyger hobbled towards the girls, wincing in pain. Her bandaged ankle was throbbing.

'You sit down there, Tyger,' the old woman ordered, and turned back to Millie and Alice-Miranda. 'She can't go anywhere, not with a sprain as bad as that.'

Millie poked her head outside the front door and scanned the landscape. She spied a light way off in the distance. 'They're coming,' she called.

'We've got two ponies.' Alice-Miranda's eyes were like dinner plates. 'We can ride double.'

The old woman frowned. 'What? You're not expecting me to go with you?'

'It's not safe here,' the child said, shaking her head. 'Those men are dangerous.'

'I've got Boomer and that old shotgun,' the woman said.

Tyger drew in a deep breath. 'You don't want to shoot anyone, and I'm pretty sure things would have got real bad if I hadn't made a run for it.'

'We can't go back the way we came,' Millie said. 'They'll see us.'

'We've come from the camp site. We're involved with the film,' Alice-Miranda explained.

The old woman nodded. 'I know another way.

313

It's steeper and it won't be fast, but I don't think they'll try to follow.'

'We've got to get moving,' Alice-Miranda urged, and then realised she hadn't even introduced herself. 'By the way, I'm Alice-Miranda Highton-Smith-Kennington-Jones and this is Millicent Jane McLoughlin-McTavish-McNoughton-McGill.'

The old woman tried to stifle a smile. 'Wow, those Hollywood names are getting longer and longer these days. I'm Aislin Devine.'

'Oh, they're not Hollywood names,' Millie said. 'Those are our real names, and you can call me Millie.'

The woman's name rolled around in Alice-Miranda's head. Devine – she'd seen it somewhere else not long ago. 'It's lovely to meet you, Miss Devine, but we really should get going.'

Millie unhitched the ponies, holding them right by the veranda so it would be easier for the ladies to hop on. Aislin threw her leg over the animal as if it were something she might have done many times before, although not for quite some time.

Alice-Miranda helped Tyger onto Patch, who stood as quietly as a mouse.

'My camera! I can't leave it here,' Tyger said, slipping sideways.

'Stay there,' Alice-Miranda ordered. 'I'll fetch it. It was on the settee, wasn't it?'

'Yes,' the woman said. 'And my book. It's in the Finkelstein's bag.'

Boomer looked at his owner and yawned, creating a noise that almost sounded like a question.

'Did that dog just ask if he could come too?' Millie stared at the beast.

'I do believe that was exactly what Boomer said,' Aislin replied proudly. 'Yes, Boom. But no chasing the wildlife, okay?'

Alice-Miranda raced inside the house and found what she was looking for. As she picked it up, the plastic shopping bag slid off the top and Tyger's book flew across the floor and lay open on the ground. She went to pick it up and another smaller book fell out of the middle. Alice-Miranda gasped. She opened the smaller book and realised that it was a journal hidden inside the hollowed-out hardback. The handwriting swirled on the page. She read the first few lines, then quickly turned back to the beginning.

'So that's it,' she said to herself. 'But why?' Alice-Miranda swiftly returned the journal to its hiding spot and into the plastic bag. She zipped up her jacket and bolted out the front door with the camera bag over her shoulder. A light flickered in the distance and the sound of an engine sliced through the still night air.

She pulled the front door shut at Miss Devine's behest and leapt onto Patch, wedging the camera bag between her and Tyger.

'I know what they were after,' she said, twisting around to face the woman. 'It's not a book. It's a journal and it was in there.'

Tyger had no idea what she was talking about. 'I bought that book a couple of weeks ago and thought I'd lost it.'

'I don't know how you got this one, but it's not yours and there's a very good reason the owner wants it back,' Alice-Miranda said, as she gathered up the reins.

Millie urged her pony to walk on and Miss Devine lit the way with a torch. 'We can only have this on for a little while otherwise they'll know where we are.'

'Okay, we've got to hurry,' Millie said, and Tonto picked up pace. They trotted around to the rear of the property just as they heard the sound of tyres crunching over the gravel out front.

Chapter 44

It was after nine o'clock when the children called it a night. Emmy appeared, following the interminably long production meeting, and suggested the group head off to bed. No one objected as they were completely exhausted and tomorrow they were due to shoot the stampede through the town, the thought of which was hair-raising and exhilarating. She was wondering where Mr Lipp had disappeared to and later found him with Frau Furtwangler, checking the set-up in her mobile recording studio.

Jacinta tapped on Alice-Miranda and Millie's bedroom door, but when there was no answer, she assumed that the girls were already asleep and made her way to bed. She drifted off as soon as her head hit the pillow and didn't stir until the morning.

Meanwhile, her best friends were bareback riding in the dark, down a mountainside so steep only the most surefooted of beasts would be capable of managing such a feat.

'Where are you taking us?' Millie asked the old woman perched behind her.

'There are no roads over this side until you get close to the location where you're filming, so those knuckleheads can't come after us in the car. They'll have to go back the long way and they'll think we're going to the camp site, but if we go to the set then you should be safe,' Miss Devine said.

Boomer ran on ahead of the group, doubling back every now and again to check they were all right. It was slow going, not more than a fast walk and, even then, there were times the girls and women held their breath as the trail slipped from underneath them and the ponies had to leap to regain their footing. On several occasions the night noises caused Millie to catch her breath too.

'Do you think they could be following us?' the girl asked at one point, when it sounded as though something had fallen from high on the ridge.

'They'd be mad,' Miss Devine said, and shifted her position behind Millie. 'I'd forgotten what a challenge bareback riding was. Not enough padding these days, I'm afraid.' The woman leaned around Millie and flashed her torch for just a second. 'There's a place we can stop beyond those boulders to give the ponies some water and a rest.'

'Out here?' Millie was sceptical. 'Are you sure that's wise?'

They wound around the edge of the hillside to where a ledge jutted out into the trail. Millie rode up to the edge and Miss Devine used it to step off Tonto's back.

'I'm not sure if I get off that I'll be able to get back on again,' Tyger said, wincing.

'Me too, dear,' the old woman said, echoing her sentiment.

Tyger threw her leg over and slipped down to the ground, flinching as the pain in her ankle took hold. She didn't want to look at it – it felt about the size of a beachball.

Miss Devine turned on the torch again and shone it against the side of the mountain.

'There's a cave!' Alice-Miranda exclaimed.

'Bring the ponies inside and I'll get them something to drink,' Miss Devine instructed. Boomer was sniffing about and disturbed a creature at the back. There was a scuffle and the girls leapt in fright as a raccoon scurried across the floor and out into the night, clearly unhappy at having been woken.

The old woman found what she was looking for – a battered tin chest, which she prised open and pulled a plastic container from. She then took out a bucket and filled it with water, which Patch and Tonto slurped faster than she could supply.

She reached back into the trunk and retrieved a small, shiny flask, which she passed to the girls. Millie hesitated. She sniffed the open container before pressing it to her lips and taking a few sips. The cool water was the best thing she'd ever tasted. Alice-Miranda was next, then handed the flask to Tyger, who had sat down on a large rock near the entrance to the cave.

'How do you know about this place?' Alice-Miranda asked.

'I put this stuff here a long time ago and every now and then I come to refill the water bottles – you never know when you might need a shelter from a storm – or a hideout from some bad guys.' Aislin's lips quivered and Alice-Miranda thought she could detect a cheeky grin. 'I've got a couple more torches, but I think it's best we don't light things up too much.'

'I think I'd rather not know what else is in here. One cranky raccoon is enough for me,' Millie said, and rubbed her aching backside. 'What time is it?'

Miss Devine looked at her watch. 'It's almost three.'

'No wonder I'm so tired,' Millie yawned.

'I think we should rest here a while, then set out again before dawn. I don't think they're following us,' Miss Devine said.

'Are you sure that we'll be safe?' Tyger Lombardi felt her stomach clench at the thought of the man who'd kidnapped her.

'I'll keep watch,' the old woman said. 'But you girls get some shut-eye.'

Alice-Miranda didn't know how she'd be able to sleep – there were so many thoughts swirling around in her head. When she'd realised the lengths the owner of that journal was prepared to take to get it back, she felt sick. Why did people have to be so complicated? She needed to talk to Uncle Lawrence as soon as she could.

Aislin Devine pulled some old blankets from the trunk. Patch and Tonto stood in the corner of the cave, their eyes already closed.

'It's not fair for you to have to stay awake, Miss Devine,' Alice-Miranda said, as the woman draped a blanket over Millie and Tyger.

'I'm fine. Now, you get some rest too, young lady,' the woman instructed.

Alice-Miranda lay down on the cold ground and closed her eyes. She was almost asleep when she remembered where she'd seen that name. 'You're not related to Maura Devine, are you?'

Aislin felt a shiver run the length of her spine. 'No, I don't know who you're talking about,' she replied, and walked to the cave entrance to gaze out upon the starlit canyon. Alice-Miranda didn't see the tear slide down the woman's scarred cheek. Moments later the child was fast asleep.

It only seemed like she was out for seconds when Miss Devine was shaking her awake. 'Girls, it's time to get up. We've got to make a move,' the old woman whispered.

Millie rolled over and sat up, rubbing her eyes. Tyger stretched and felt the throb of her ankle.

Miss Devine turned from the mouth of the cave. 'Seems I underestimated those fellas.'

'What?' Millie was on her feet, helping Alice-Miranda to hers. 'Are they out there?'

Aislin pointed to a light on the hillside. 'They're a ways off, but we might be in trouble once dawn breaks.'

Alice-Miranda quickly folded the blankets and stuffed them into the trunk, along with the other equipment.

'Tell me you didn't just do that?' Millie shook her head.

Alice-Miranda shrugged. 'I can't help it.'

'A girl after my own heart,' Miss Devine said, smiling.

Using the tin box to stand on, the foursome mounted the ponies and were out of the cave before they saw the flashlight on the hillside again. Boomer led the way down the mountain trail as the first rays of morning sun speared across the valley.

Alice-Miranda gasped. 'It's beautiful.'

323

'Wow!' Millie said. It almost didn't seem real.

Tyger Lombardi held on to her camera bag and wished they had time to stop. 'Maybe this is what I should be taking photographs of,' she murmured.

The comment made Alice-Miranda smile, but the peace was shattered by an angry voice.

'I can see you, Tyger Lombardi!' a man yelled.

Millie looked across the ravine. 'How far away is he?'

'A couple o' miles as the buzzard flies, but we'd best get a kick along,' Miss Devine said. Aided by the morning light, the ponies picked up their pace, leaving the tall man further behind. He seemed to be on his own. Who knew what he'd done with his offsider?

Chapter 45

'What do you mean you haven't seen them since last night?' Emmy gasped.

Mr Lipp felt faint and he mopped at the cold sweat on his brow. 'What about this morning?' he rasped. 'Surely you saw them this morning?'

Jacinta shook her head. 'I just thought they must have left early and hadn't wanted to wake me.'

'Well, we've got to find them.' Harold Lipp grasped the lapels of his pony-patterned waistcoat.

He'd chosen it especially for today, as a nod to the upcoming stampede sequence.

The trio raced off the bus to the girls' trailer. Emmy pulled open the wardrobe door and let out a strangled cry. There, hanging pristinely, were Alice-Miranda's and Millie's costumes. The woman's stomach clenched and she thought she was going to throw up. Mr Lipp was as pale as a piece of paper. And things were only about to get worse when they ran back to the bus and were confronted by Miss Connie, who declared that two of her ponies were missing. Patch and Tonto – the ponies Alice-Miranda and Millie had been riding the day before.

'I thought they were lovely girls,' the woman said in her southern drawl. 'But clearly they're Hollywood brats! Stealing my horses. You wait until I get my hands on them.'

Mr Lipp shook his head violently. 'I can assure you that neither one of those girls is anything like a brat.' He lowered his voice and added, 'I mean, if it had been Caprice who was missing with a pony, well, one might have expected such a thing, but not Alice-Miranda and Millie.'

'We've got to do something,' Lucas said. 'What about a helicopter search party?'

Emmy nodded. 'That's a great idea, although there are none here at the moment. Alexa and Lawrence are due back any minute now, and so are Mrs Goldberg and Mrs Crawford, and I think Mr Goldberg is flying out this morning too. We'll have three of them here soon, but we need to do something before then.'

Emmy had already called the site manager, who had every one of his staff members scouring the camp for the missing girls. Minutes later the man reappeared at the bus with a grave look on his face, shaking his head.

'Would they have taken the ponies and ridden out to the location?' the man asked.

'I doubt it,' Mr Lipp said. He was doing his best to contain the vortex of worrying thoughts inside his head. 'Something has happened. Those two are the most reliable girls I know.'

'I think it's worth a chance going out there,' Emmy said. 'Come on.'

The group boarded the bus and the driver fired up the engine. Miss Connie had already sent the rest of her team ahead with the horses, otherwise she was going to suggest that a search party on four legs would move faster than two. If the girls weren't at the location, that's what they'd do. The woman's forehead resembled several rows of purl-stitch knitting. She was thinking about something she'd overheard last night. Miss Connie leaned in and whispered to Emmy, not wanting to alarm everyone else if it turned out to be nothing. But from the look on the young woman's face, they had to find those girls and fast.

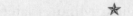

The ponies jogged down the mountain, sidestepping and leaping over rocks and stones to keep their riders safe.

Millie squinted into the distance. She pointed to a cluster of man-made structures and saw a trail of dust from a vehicle. 'Is that the set?'

Miss Devine nodded. 'Not far now.'

'It's still miles away,' the child said, her heart sinking.

Tyger Lombardi swivelled her head to see if he'd gained ground. 'Faster, girls, he's so close!' she shouted.

Miss Devine clung to Millie's middle and Tyger held fast to Alice-Miranda.

'You're not going to get away with this!' he yelled, his voice bouncing off the hills.

Tyger gripped her camera bag as they rounded another bend in the trail and were confronted by a giant boulder.

The horses whinnied and slid to a halt.

'What are we going to do?' Millie turned to the old woman behind her.

'There's another way. We'll have to double back and take the trail further to the east,' Aislin said.

Alice-Miranda wheeled Patch around and Millie followed suit. Boomer led the way. For a second they caught sight of their hunter. He looked much closer than he'd been before. Having to retrace their steps was problematic as he hadn't yet passed the fork in the trail.

'Hurry, girls,' the old woman breathed. 'Hurry!'

Chapter 46

The bus was engulfed by a cloud of dust as it pulled up to the set. Emmy had tried to make several calls on the way out, but couldn't get any service. She asked Mr Lipp to keep the children calm and on the bus while she raced off to find Andreas King, who'd been on location since before dawn. Today was the most important day of the shoot, considering the complexity of an action sequence that involved twenty buffalo and a posse of child riders. Although the enormous scale of the scene would mostly play out with the aid of computer-generated imagery, Andreas was anxious nonetheless. The action involved children and he couldn't afford for there to be any mishaps.

He'd checked and rechecked the generator, the cables, the cameras, the set and anything else he thought could possibly go wrong.

'Mr King,' Emmy called out to the man. He was concentrating on the notes in his folder, which he hadn't let out of his sight since the day before. 'We have a problem.'

The man's face dropped. 'But I've checked everything. I've been out here since four,' he said, looking as if he were about to cry. 'This film's a disaster!'

'Please calm down.' Emmy patted his arm. 'I'm sure that we'll find them, but Alice-Miranda and Millie and two of the ponies are missing.'

'What?!' Andreas immediately snapped out of his petulant strop. 'What do you mean they're missing? Why would they take off? I can't believe it. They're not the only ones, you know. Donny, my sometimes driver, is gone too. He was here yesterday, went up with me in the chopper and I asked him to give me a hand this morning, but he hasn't turned up.'

Emmy's heart skipped a beat. If that was true, then what Miss Connie had overheard was most likely right. 'I don't think the girls have taken off. I think they're in trouble,' Emmy said.

The gravity of the situation was beginning to dawn on the young man. 'We're at the Grand Canyon,' he said. 'It's dangerous out here. We've got to find them. Those kids are probably my responsibility. You know I'm too young for this much stress.'

The man ran to his makeshift work station. He picked up the satellite phone and tried to dial out, but the thing was dead. His mobile wasn't working either. Andreas bit his thumbnail and fidgeted like a five-year-old, trying to work out what they should do next.

It was Miss Connie who had a plan. She was off the bus and had all the ponies saddled and ready to head out in no time. Fortunately, her two roustabouts had tacked up most of the horses before they arrived. She raced back to the bus and asked which of the children was prepared to go with her.

When Emmy and Andreas had finally decided on a course of action, they were just in time to see Miss Connie and the children cantering away into the distance.

'Where are they going?' Emmy said, mortified.

'I – I couldn't stop them. That Miss Connie's a very persuasive woman,' Harold Lipp stammered. 'Even Sloane and Sasha have gone.'

Chapter 47

The girls reached the fork in the trail and began their descent. It was steeper on this side of the mountain and the stones were looser too, but they didn't have a choice.

'I can see him,' Tyger said. He was gaining on them as he tripped and slipped down the mountain. 'He's coming!'

The ponies picked up their pace. Alice-Miranda could see the bottom, where the ground levelled off.

'Hang on, Miss Lombardi! Lean back!' she

ordered, and kicked her little paint beast in the flank. 'Yah!' she cried, and the pony began to run. The tiny child clung to the animal's bare coat. It was a miracle that the two of them stayed on. Patch made one almighty leap to the level ground below, just as the man tripped and rolled past them. He had tried to grab the pony's tail on his way down, but Alice-Miranda had manoeuvred the beast out of the way in the nick of time.

Bruised and bleeding, the man slowly got to his feet. He spat something out of his mouth and coughed.

Millie and Miss Devine had reached the bottom of the hill too. Boomer bounded towards the fellow, who kicked out, connecting with the old dog's ribs and causing him to yelp in pain. Alice-Miranda felt a shift beneath her as she pushed Patch on, but the pony was hobbling.

'He's lame,' Alice-Miranda said. 'We can't go any further.'

The problem was that Tyger Lombardi was lame too. Her ankle was still throbbing and she knew that once she was off the horse she was a sitting duck.

'Be careful, Alice-Miranda, that's the edge of the canyon back there,' Miss Devine called.

The child slipped down to the ground as the man circled.

'Give me that journal, Tyger. Give it to me and we can cut a deal,' he demanded.

'Why should I? You do realise you had it all along when you took my camera bag,' the woman said.

'What?' He looked at her incredulously. 'So you knew about it and you've been lying to me this whole time?'

Tyger shook her head. 'I had no idea and I still don't know what it is exactly or where it came from. Alice-Miranda found it in the bag. I thought it was the novel I'd been missing.'

He eyeballed the tiny child with the chocolate curls. If she'd read it, he was done for. 'Give it to me and I'll let you go,' he said. If he could deliver it to the owner, he could still collect the money and be out of the country by nightfall.

'No!' Alice-Miranda stood her ground. 'You're not going to get away with this.'

The man lunged at Tyger, who was holding the bag. 'Give it to me!' He snatched it, but she held on tight. The pair of them rolled over and over, trying to take the prize.

Alice-Miranda ran towards them and kicked

the bag away. The man made one last grab, but it flew out over the edge of the canyon.

'Nooooooo!' he shouted, and dove after it. In one heart-stopping moment, the man lost his balance and toppled sideways, disappearing over the rim.

The children and Miss Devine gasped. The woman cradled her face in her hands. There would be only one outcome.

'My camera!' Tyger watched on in horror as the bag plummeted to the bottom of the ravine, almost two kilometres below. There was a thump and a thud, but it was too loud and too soon to be the bag.

'Help me!' the man called. Alice-Miranda raced to the edge and peered over.

Not far below them, on a small ledge, the man was lying facedown. He moaned and shifted his leg.

'He's alive!' Alice-Miranda exclaimed.

Millie's heart was pounding and she felt faint. 'I can't look,' she said, covering her eyes.

The sound of pounding hooves momentarily diverted their attention as the girls were stunned to see a cavalry charging towards them.

'There they are!' Jacinta shouted.

'Help!' Millie cried as she slowly backed Tonto away from the edge. She and Miss Devine slipped off the pony's back and the old woman took the reins, leading him from harm's way.

Alice-Miranda looked around for something she could throw to the man, but there was nothing. As the riders reached them, there was a loud cheer.

Miss Connie leapt from her mount and ran to the child. 'You're safe!' She wrapped her wiry arms around the girl.

'Yes, but he's not,' Alice-Miranda said, pointing to the cliff's edge.

Jacinta dismounted and ran to hug her friends and the others soon surrounded them too.

The man on the ledge moaned. 'Help me.'

For a split second, Tyger Lombardi thought she might be very happy to leave him there, given what he had intended for her.

'Please,' he sobbed. 'I don't want to die. I was stupid and greedy.'

'We need to make a chain,' Alice-Miranda ordered.

Miss Connie ran to her saddle and grabbed a long loop of thick rope, which she quickly tied to the pommel. She pulled the pony away from the edge and threw the other end to Alice-Miranda, who guided it down to the man.

He had managed to get himself upright and was clinging to the cliff face. Alice-Miranda told him to loop it around his middle and grip it further up. His fingers fumbled until he finally tied the knot.

'We all need to pull,' Alice-Miranda instructed.

Lucas, Blade and Sasha were the first behind her. She grabbed on to the rope and the boys held on to her. The rest of the children formed a human chain, each taking up a position along the line. Miss Connie urged her pony backwards as the children heaved and hauled, inching the man up the precipice. They gasped and held their breath when he slipped a couple of times, sending a spray of stones showering below, but he eventually reached the top. Alice-Miranda and Lucas lay on their stomachs as they pulled him over the edge to safety.

He was on the ground, puffing and panting.

'Tie him up,' Tyger ordered.

'Donny?' Blade's eyes widened. 'He's our driver – well, sometimes. Him and the short, fat guy Joe.'

'Put a sock in it, kid,' the man growled. 'You and that painful mother of yours. And tell her she had better give that money back too, seeing that you and Sasha have done a deal to switch parts.'

'What money?' Blade frowned. The group looked

at each other, wondering what Donny was talking about. Then it dawned on Blade why his mother had been acting so strangely about him having the lead role. He was disappointed but understood this wasn't just about him. There was his family to think about too.

Sasha and Lucas grabbed the rope and bound the man's hands and legs.

'Helicopters!' Sophie pointed in the distance as three choppers appeared on the horizon.

Minutes later they landed one by one, with Lawrence out first, followed by Alexa. Aviva Goldberg and Tish Crawford were next, then Eli Goldberg appeared with his mother and father. Andreas King arrived soon after with Emmy and Mr Lipp in a four-wheel drive.

Lawrence spied Tyger, battered and bruised, sitting on the ground. 'What's all this?' he said, kneeling down. 'You said you were fine and had gone away.'

Tyger pointed at Donny. 'He sent the message when he kidnapped me and stole my phone.'

Abe and Dinah Goldberg reached the group and, from the looks on their faces, were both stunned by the scene in front of them.

'I'm cancelling the movie,' Abe said, his eyes glistening. 'It *is* cursed. I should never have thought I could make everything okay.'

Dinah looked at her husband. 'What are you talking about, Abe? Okay how?'

'Mr Goldberg, I can assure you the movie is not cursed. Someone close to you wanted this movie to fail to force your retirement,' Alice-Miranda explained. She unzipped her jacket to reveal a hardback book. An Agatha Christie classic. 'Mrs Goldberg, I believe this belongs to you.'

Dinah gasped, her hand clutching at her chest. She shook her head and glanced at her husband, then quickly turned away. 'Oh, Abe, I am so ashamed,' she said, her voice trembling. 'Can you ever forgive me for what I've done?'

The cast and crew were spellbound, anxious to know what was going to happen next.

'I read it,' Aislin said from the other side of the group. 'I think there might have been better ways to get the desired outcome, but I understand.' The crowd parted as Miss Devine walked towards the Goldbergs. 'You were afraid that something terrible would happen, just like what happened to me.'

'Maura!' Abe breathed. For a moment, he seemed to have had the wind knocked clean out of him.

'Of course,' Alice-Miranda whispered.

'I haven't gone by that name for more than half a century,' Aislin said, her eyes shiny with tears.

Dinah's face crumpled and she put her hands to her mouth. 'But you died and it was all my fault.'

'Maura died but Aislin lived,' the woman said. 'I spent years being angry with you. You ruined my career, you took the love of my life from me. I moved out here not to forget but to remember. Every single day. But over time it didn't matter any more. I liked it – the isolation, the emptiness. By the time my scars faded, Maura had disappeared and I had no desire to ever go back. The accident wasn't your fault, Dinah. It was mine and deep down I always knew that.'

Tears welled in Abe Goldberg's eyes. He brushed them away. 'I searched for you,' he said. 'For years, I had investigators looking.'

Aislin nodded. 'It was lucky I made some money in the movies, because whatever you were paying them, I paid more. When I found out that Cecil had died, it was far better that I stayed away from the Goldbergs forever. You need to read this.' Aislin took the journal from Alice-Miranda and passed it to the man. 'Not a day has gone by that Dinah hasn't blamed herself for the accident and yet it wasn't her fault. The reason she didn't want you to make this film was because of the memories. Your brother, the love of my life, died that day. Making it fail meant Eli could finally take over and she could have some time with you. You need to do that, Abe. She loves you, and the one thing you still have is time.'

Alice-Miranda wiped at her eyes. Miss Devine did too.

'If it wasn't for these two brave little girls, who knows what would have happened out there last night,' Miss Devine said.

'Oh, Maura.' Dinah Goldberg rushed to her sister-in-law and the two of them hugged tightly.

Abe Goldberg turned and looked at the cast and crew. 'I don't know. Should we do this thing or not?'

Sasha steeled himself. 'Only if Blade can play the lead.'

Aviva glowered. 'Booboola, what do you mean?'

'Mum, I never wanted to be in this movie in the first place,' Sasha said, trying to be brave. 'I only auditioned because I wanted to make you proud. But I should never have got the part, right, Grandma?'

Dinah stepped back from Aislin and nodded. 'Probably not,' she said. 'Oh, what am I saying? Never in a million years.'

'Thank heavens for that,' Abe said. 'Your singing is worse than Charlotte Highton-Smith's – no offence, Lawrence, but that wife of yours cannot carry a tune.'

'But I don't think Blade should be the lead,' Tish Crawford said.

Everyone stared at her.

'Yes, he should,' Caprice said. 'He's really talented.' She looked at the boy and smiled. Blade felt his heart skip a beat.

Dinah Goldberg sighed. 'You can keep the money and I'll make sure that Blade gets paid the rest of what he's owed.'

All eyes switched to Dinah – she certainly had done her best to make sure the movie was a disaster.

'Well, we'd better get back to the set,' Andreas said, and flinched as his headset buzzed. 'What do you mean someone let the buffalo loose?' he screamed.

Dinah walked over to him. 'Ask them to find Joe and keep him locked up until we get there,' she said calmly. 'I think you'll find *he's* the curse. And you had better send your grandmother the biggest bunch of flowers you can afford when you get back to the city – to thank her for getting you this job.'

Eli grimaced at his mother, realising Andreas was yet another part of her grand plan to bring the movie unstuck.

'As for you,' Dinah said, turning to Donny. 'Five million dollars? You told me that's what Tyger was asking for as payment for my journal. I have a feeling you might have been exaggerating.'

'Exaggerating!' Tyger huffed. 'I didn't even know I had it.' She stood up and hobbled over to Donny. Then, balancing on her sore foot, she kicked his shin with her good leg as hard as she could.

'Ow!' Donny yelped.

'He was going to take the money and throw me off the edge of the canyon,' Tyger continued, and kicked him again for good measure.

'Ow! Seriously?' he whined.

'And I believe he and his friend were planning to flee to Costa Rica, or was it Rio?' Alice-Miranda glared at the man.

'Miss Lombardi, I had no idea. My behaviour has been appalling.' Dinah pressed her lips tightly together.

Abe walked over to his wife. 'I'm sorry you've blamed yourself for all these years,' he said softly.

'I'm the one who should be sorry. What was I thinking? I've put so many people in danger. Miss Lombardi could have been killed because of my selfishness. Can you ever forgive me?' she said, taking his hands in hers.

Abe Goldberg wrapped his arms around the woman he loved and hugged her tightly.

Alice-Miranda walked over and looked up at Miss Devine. 'I saw a picture of you in the Goldbergs' attic. You were lovely.'

The woman's violet eyes sparkled. 'Not so much now.'

The child slipped her hand into hers. 'Every single bit.'

And just in case you're wondering . . .

Abe Goldberg decided that *Frontier Woman: The Life and Times of Nellie Williams* would be his last film as Head of Goldberg Studios. He passed the baton to his son, who was thrilled to finally be given the opportunity. Aviva Goldberg could not be prouder that her husband is now in charge of Goldberg Studios. She's already set about redecorating the offices and entrance gates. She has one theme in mind – bling!

The rest of the shoot went off without a hitch. Alice-Miranda and her friends had a wonderful time, and the buffalo scene, though challenging, proved to be great fun. Filming wrapped three months later. It's currently in post-production and looks to be one of the highlights of the year. Andreas King can't quite believe that his name is being thrown around as a contender for awards season. Grizelda Furtwangler, on the other hand, is counting on it.

Harold Lipp hasn't told anyone yet, but he's been busy applying for jobs in Hollywood, hoping that he and Frau Furtwangler will soon be together permanently. Alice-Miranda didn't forget about a special souvenir for Mr Trout and arranged to get a framed photograph of the children on set. Actually, she got two – one of them looking fabulous and the other in their alien make-up. Mr Trout adored them both.

At Abe Goldberg's insistence, Tish Crawford and her entire family have moved into the third residence on the Goldberg property. While Blade and his mother were away in the desert, Ray Crawford had received an offer for the farm that he couldn't refuse. While he loved the land, he hated farming and had only gone into the family business because he thought it would make his father proud. What he was really interested in was sound production. He'd secretly been doing a correspondence course for the past couple of years in the hopes that one day the whole family would move to Hollywood. Sasha and Blade are the best of friends and Tish and Aviva are inseparable.

Caprice is relishing her star status and can't wait until the movie's release, although her mother has decided this will be her one and only feature role until she finishes school. She's still trying to work out if Blade hates her or wants to marry her.

Donny and Joe are currently in prison, having been charged with kidnapping and extortion among a slew of other offences. Dinah Goldberg had no idea of Donny's plan to do away with Tyger and take the money for himself. Joe had been sabotaging all manner of things on set, but he flatly denied having anything to do with the Oompa Loompa make-up fiasco or the buffalo great escape. It was lucky for Dinah that Tyger refused to press any charges against the woman, knowing the turmoil she'd been through.

Aislin Devine's movie career was cut short when a huge explosion occurred on the set of the original version of *Frontier Woman: The Life and Times of Nellie Williams*. She and her husband, Cecil Goldberg, the director and Abe's older brother, were among the victims. Dinah Goldberg had always believed that it had been her fault when she'd lit a cigarette on set, but the spark had actually been caused by the static from Aislin's dress. Cecil was killed and Aislin was left horribly scarred. She retreated to the other side of the world to recuperate before returning to the desert, where they had been supposed to shoot the second half of the film. Abe had vowed that, one day, *The Life and Times of Nellie Williams* would make it to the silver screen in honour of Cecil and his wife.

Aislin declined her sister-in-law's offer to stay with them in Hollywood, but she invited Dinah and Abe to visit her at the canyon, which, surprisingly, they did.

Millie and Sasha have been trading letters every other week. She's hoping that he might do an exchange to Fayle very soon. In the meantime, inspired by their make-up debacle on set, Millie is busy writing her first screenplay with the working title *Cowgirls and Aliens: Extra-terrestrials of the Wild West*.

Meanwhile, Sasha has discovered a love of tinkering. His father owned an old racing car and, with Blade and Sophie as his assistants, Sasha has just got it going again. He's planning to learn to drive it very soon.

Lawrence is looking forward to spending some time at home with Charlotte and the twins before his next project, although he's worried that Magdalena has been cooking so much that he'll have to spend twice as long in the gym to maintain his physique. At Venetia Baldini's insistence, Magdalena is putting together her first Mexican recipe book. She's trying to decide on a title, but *Chilli Business: Cooking with the Fire* is her current favourite.

Tyger came to possess Dinah's journal due to a simple mix-up at her birthday lunch. The two women were seated at adjacent tables when the waiter had dropped that tray. Dinah had taken her journal with her, popping it into a Finkelstein's bag, because she only ever wrote in it away from the house. She'd come up with an ingenious way of concealing her many years' worth of writing inside the Agatha Christie books her husband loathed. There was never any danger of him finding them – or so she thought. When the waiter had cleared up the mess, he'd handed the women the wrong bags. Dinah knew who Tyger was because of Charlotte

Highton-Smith's encounter with the paparazzo. Charlotte had shown her the woman's picture in case Dinah spotted her anywhere near the house.

Alice-Miranda managed to have a quiet chat with Abe Goldberg about Tyger Lombardi, telling the man how brave the woman had been and that perhaps her photography skills could be put to better use with a little bit of help. The Goldbergs purchased Tyger a state-of-the-art camera with the biggest and best lenses on the market and offered her a fabulous new job to go with it. She's loving her role as the official photographer of Goldberg Studios.

Glossary of film terminology

armourer   film crew specialist, sometimes known as the weapons master, in charge of weapons

best boy (lighting)   assistant to the head of the lighting department, not to be confused with best boy (grip)

boom   a microphone often attached to a pole

boom operator   the person who holds the boom, ensuring it is as close to the actors as possible

call sheet   the schedule created by the assistant director, allowing the cast and crew to know where they need to be and when

CGI computer-generated imagery

clapperboard a device used to assist in the synchronising of picture and sound and to mark particular scenes and takes

dialect coach an acting coach who works with the actors to create the voice and speech of the character, including any accents

director gives direction to the cast and crew and creates an overall vision for the film

director of photography oversees the camera work

executive producer finances the film and makes sure they have the money to make it

first assistant director manages the daily progress of the film, arranging logistics, checking on the cast and crew, and preparing daily call sheets (this is a big job!)

gaffer head of the lighting department

grip camera and rigging technician

head wrangler provides and manages animals such as horses and buffalo, as well as riders, that are specially trained in stunt work

location the place where filming occurs away from the movie studio

make-up supervisor oversees the make-up and is in charge of the entire department

musical director   responsible for the musical aspects of a performance or production

on-set dresser   works with the set dressing team but remains on set during the filming to ensure that the small details of the set are in place, such as curtains and door handles

post-production   the stage after filming where processes such as editing, sound design, colour correction and the addition of visual special effects are carried out

rushes   the raw film footage from a day's shoot, also known as the 'dailies' or 'daily rushes'

sound stage   a soundproof hangar-like building

stunt double   a body double to replace the actors during especially dangerous or difficult scenes

take   refers to each filmed version of a particular shot or set-up. Takes of each shot are generally numbered, starting from 'take one' and the number of each successive take is increased (with the director calling for 'take two', 'take three' and so on) until the filming of the shot is completed

video assist operator   operates and troubleshoots a complex system of equipment (including monitors, recorders and hundreds of metres of cable) that allows the film-maker to view a scene immediately after shooting it

wardrobe mistress   an early Hollywood term for the person in charge of the costume department, more often referred to as a costume supervisor these days

Cast of characters

Winchesterfield-Downsfordvale students

Alice-Miranda Highton-Smith-Kennington-Jones — Only child, nine years of age

Millicent Jane McLoughlin-McTavish-McNoughton-McGill — Alice-Miranda's best friend and room mate

Jacinta Headlington-Bear — Friend

Sloane Sykes — Friend

Caprice Radford — Friend of sorts

Fayle School for Boys staff and students

Mr Harold Lipp — English and Drama teacher

Lucas Nixon — Alice-Miranda's cousin

Septimus Sykes — Lucas's best friend and brother of Sloane

***Frontier Woman: The Life and Times of Nellie Williams* cast and crew**

Lawrence Ridley — Famous movie actor and Aunt Charlotte's husband

Abe Goldberg — Head of Goldberg Studios

Eli Goldberg — Executive of Goldberg Studios

Andreas King	Director
Emmy	First assistant director
Jerome Menzel	Director of hair and make-up
Mrs Sparrow	Wardrobe mistress
Grizelda Furtwangler	Musical director
Wade Riley	Script coach
Hannah	Dialect coach
Miss Connie	Head wrangler
Sasha Goldberg	Not-so-aspiring actor, son of Eli and Aviva
Blade Crawford	Child actor
Sophie Roussos	Child actor
Dylan	Chief of security
Patch	Alice-Miranda's pony
Tonto	Millie's pony

Others

Charlotte Highton-Smith	Alice-Miranda's aunt
Marcus and Imogen Ridley	Twin toddlers of Charlotte and Lawrence
Magdalena	Charlotte and Lawrence's cook
Venetia Baldini	Beloved television chef and Caprice's mother
Dinah Goldberg	Wife of Abe and mother of Eli
Aviva Goldberg	Wife of Eli and mother of Sasha
Tish Crawford	Blade's mother
Bob Loy	Lawrence's driver
Tyger Lombardi	Hollywood paparazzo
Aislin Devine	Recluse
Boomer	Aislin's faithful bloodhound
Garber Sheedy	Delivery man
Anders	Tyger's neighbour

About the Author

Jacqueline Harvey taught for many years in girls' boarding schools. She is the author of the bestselling Alice-Miranda series and the Clementine Rose series, and was awarded Honour Book in the 2006 Australian CBC Awards for her picture book *The Sound of the Sea*. She now writes full-time and is working on more Alice-Miranda and Clementine Rose adventures as well as an exciting new series.

www.jacquelineharvey.com.au

Jacqueline
Supports

Jacqueline Harvey is a passionate educator who enjoys sharing her love of reading and writing with children and adults alike. She is an ambassador for Dymocks Children's Charities and Room to Read. Find out more at www.dcc.gofundraise.com.au and www.roomtoread.org.